DARK SECRETS

Recent Titles by Peter Turnbull

AFTER THE FLOOD *
AND DID MURDER HIM
CONDITION PURPLE
DEATHTRAP *
KILLING FLOOR
LONG DAY MONDAY
THE MAN WITH NO FACE
PERILS AND DANGERS *
THE RETURN *
TWO WAY CUT

* *available from Severn House*

DARK SECRETS

Peter Turnbull

This first world edition published in Great Britain 2002 by
SEVERN HOUSE PUBLISHERS LTD of
9–15 High Street, Sutton, Surrey SM1 1DF.
This first world edition published in the USA 2003 by
SEVERN HOUSE PUBLISHERS INC of
595 Madison Avenue, New York, N.Y. 10022.

Copyright © 2002 by Peter Turnbull.

British Library Cataloguing in Publication Data

Turnbull, Peter, 1950-
    Dark secrets
    1.   Hennessey, Chief Inspector (Fictitious character) - Fiction
    2.   Yellich, Sergeant (Fictitious character) - Fiction
    3.   Police - England - Yorkshire - Fiction
    4.   Detective and mystery stories
    I.   Title
    823.9'14 [F]

    ISBN 0-7278-5908-0

Printed and bound in Great Britain by
MPG Books Ltd., Bodmin, Cornwall.

One

*. . . in which a tale of loss and recovery is related,
and a field and a house give up their secrets.*

To an observer he appeared thus. A short, overweight male, well below average height, of round, ruddy complexion, clean-shaven save for a trimmed moustache. He wore baggy denims and training shoes, a donkey jacket, with a canvas knapsack slung round his neck, rather than rifle-like from his shoulder, and upon his head was a cloth cap on to which he had pinned many small, coloured badges of the sort that children attach to their clothing. He tended to walk with what would appear to the observer as a rolling gait, staggering slightly, placing the weight of his body wholly on one foot, then the other; and yet effecting a forward momentum. His eyes would appear bleary and bloodshot. He was a man to look at once and then forget. An ambling, shuffling drunkard. Not quite a shuffling-through-litter-bin-meths/fortified-wine drinker, but a man from whom beer and beer and beer and yet more beer had, over the years, taken her toll.

The man walked the ancient medieval streets, narrow, with overhanging houses, until he came to the wall, which he joined. He was a native of this small town with City Charter, and he knew, like all its sons and daughters, that walking the walls, wherever possible, is by far the quickest

1

way to cross the city. He joined the wall at Lendal Bridge and walked to Micklegate Bar. Other people were on the wall, tourists mostly, easily recognized by their cameras and day bags, and their looking eagerly, excitedly from side to side and by their rarely being alone: mostly they were in groups. Citizens of the town, by contrast, carried no cameras, rarely carried a bag, walked alone, and did not look from left to right. It was the latter who would often look at the man once and then dismiss him; the tourists seemed to see no other person on the wall, their focus being ancient buildings and ramparts.

The man ambled on and glanced skywards. It was, he would later recall, because this day was to be momentous in a life which he already felt to be unfulfilled, a low, grey sky and a strong wind from the north and east. Such details would stay with the man. It was mid September, unseasonably cold and dull, and that in itself seemed appropriate. The man pursued a chill purpose.

The man had done this walk before. Walking from his small, rented house into the city, then across the city to the wall, on to the wall at Lendal Bridge and leaving it again at Micklegate Bar, glanced at the police station and then balked, walked away down Micklegate, away from the police station, away from what his beer-laden conscience told him was his civic and bounden duty, and into the first pub he came to. He did that because he feared what would certainly be the first question from what was certain to be an incredulous police officer: 'Why didn't you come forward earlier?'

Why indeed? Even he didn't know the answer. But on this day, this Monday, he had awoken with a new determination. Today he would go through with it. And he left his house earlier than usual, so early that he would arrive at Micklegate Bar before the pubs were open, so that the only thing open to him would be the Victorian stone portal of Micklegate Bar Police Station. And he did it, he did it, with an unforeseen, unexpected feeling of a weight falling off him as he crossed the threshold of the police station, and also of a sense of security falling on him. He walked up to the enquiry desk where stood a young, fresh-faced constable and he said, 'I seen a woman killed.'

When the words came, finally, they came easily and the man shuddered, almost, as the tension of the last few months was released. He found time to observe that the young constable, whilst clearly not dismissing the man with badges in his cap who had walked in off the street and made a heart-stopping statement, nonetheless, showed no flicker of emotion, no sign of surprise other than perhaps, just perhaps, a slight narrowing of the eyes. 'I seen a woman killed,' he said again.

'I see, sir.' The constable reached for a pro-forma, which copied in triplicate. He was calm, unhurried. 'Can I have your name, please, sir?'

'Killed!'

'Yes, sir. Your name?'

'Henderson,' said the man, adjusting his knapsack, 'Michael Henderson.'

'Your age?'

'Fifty-four.'

'Address?' Michael Henderson gave an address in Tang Hall. 'For the moment.'

'For the moment?'

'I keep moving about, a new address every six months. Always have done, can't settle. Same pub though,' he added, focusing his eyes on the constable's pen and the notepad as if keen to confirm that all his details were being recorded accurately.

'But this is your current address?'

'Yes.'

'Alright. Could you please take a seat on that bench just there behind you. I'll ask someone to come and take a statement from you.'

Michael Henderson turned and sat, as invited, on the hard bench. It was upholstered with leather but when he sat on it, he found that it was as hard as if it was made of wood. It had impressive armrests at either end and he found time to study their ornate carvings. Then his mind once again refocused to the issue at hand. So far it had been easy, though he knew the worst was to come, but at least he had started – there was no going back now. So, whatever the reaction of the police, it meant that he was not, at least, going to take this to his grave. That had been his greatest fear, that he would die before he could tell of what he had seen.

Fifteen minutes later, Detective Sergeant Yellich looked across the table at the bleary-eyed Michael Henderson and said, 'How long ago?'

'About twenty years,' Henderson mumbled sheepishly, apologetically.

It was the reaction he had feared, and it was just as strong as he had feared it would be.

Yellich dropped his pen on the statement form and leaned back in his chair. 'But why didn't you come forward sooner?'

'Dunno . . .' Michael Henderson shrugged his shoulders. 'But, in a way, you could say it was only twelve months that I kept it to myself.'

'How so?'

'I forgot it . . . I mean it went from my mind soon after . . . almost . . . well, I can't remember, day after, two days after, it was like it hadn't happened.'

'Not helped by the alcohol, perhaps?'

'Well, that's just me, I was into my dad's home brew from the age of thirteen. It's my life. I'd die without beer, I'm killing myself with it. Some choice. So I saw what I saw, can't say for sure how long ago it was, but it was about twenty years and then I forgot it, all of it, like it had never happened. Then one day about a year ago, I was standing in the tap room of the Green Man during "happy hour" and I remembered an image . . . like I was looking at a dream . . . couldn't work out whether I was remembering a dream or whether it had happened. After that, I remembered more and more but disjointed, out of order.'

'Sequence,' Yellich said. 'Out of sequence.' He too had experienced recovered memories, he too had experienced how a memory can flood back into one's mind, initially out of sequence, but eventually it is all recovered, all details, words, smells, sounds, it's all there, crystal clear then to be recalled at will, or always there like a nagging ache. 'The word is sequence.'

'Same difference.' Michael Henderson shrugged his shoulders again. It was, Yellich was to find, a personality trait of the man, and a trait he was to find annoying, a sort of 'it's-not-my-fault' kind of a shrug. The prisons are full of folk with just such an attitude, so Yellich observed. 'Anyway, after a few more weeks there was just nothing more to remember. Then I didn't know what to do with it, the memory I mean . . . like where do I put it? Then I began to think that I can't take this to my grave and my doctor's told me I'm for the clay sooner rather than later. The drink you see.'

'I can see, yes.' Yellich stood. 'A cup of tea or coffee, I think. I'd better make your coffee black. Then we'll take all the details that you remember.'

5

'Aye.' Michael Henderson settled back in his chair and surveyed the room as Yellich stepped into the corridor to feed coins into a hot-drinks vending machine. The walls he saw were painted with two-tone brown, light over dark, they had no decoration whatsoever, and once the door was shut the room had no source of natural light. It had just a table (metal) and four chairs, metal framed with semi-upholstered seats and a wooden back rest. In his permanent state of semi-drunkenness, Michael Henderson could see that the room served to focus attention on the matter in hand. No distraction allowed.

Yellich returned and placed a white plastic beaker containing hot black liquid in front of Michael Henderson and shut the door behind him, telling Henderson to be careful because it was 'piping hot' and that he'd burn his tongue if he didn't take care. He sat opposite Henderson and put his own drink of tea, to one side. He picked up the pen and toyed with it, rather than prepared to write with it, and leaned back in his chair and invited Henderson to tell the tale in his own words.

'I was in the bushes, near the waste ground. It was about two, three a.m., dark, no moon, raining.'

'No need for me to ask what you were doing?'

'Trying to make ends meet.'

'Is one way of putting it.'

'I was going to break into a place.'

'OK.'

'The waste ground is surrounded by shrubs, then behind the shrubs in one corner, is a wire fence.'

'Where is the waste ground?'

'Out in the sticks, down a lane between York and Selby. The premises I was going to do was a car dealership, and they rented cars too. I was employed by them as a night watchie. The pay was bad, one pint of beer an hour.'

'They paid you in alcohol!'

'No, they paid enough for one pint of beer for each hour's work. How's a man going to survive?'

'How indeed?' But Yellich had to concede the rate of pay was by no means princely.

'But at least I didn't have to do much for it. Sit in a hut listening to the radio, walk about a bit if it wasn't raining. I had a phone to call the law if anything went down. The premises were, like, the storage for the dealership, they had showrooms and rental places in York and Selby and Wetherby – Mallard's, you must know them?'

'Oh, yes. Prestige cars.'

'Yes. Second-hand cars but very nice, Rolls, Bentleys, BMWs, and if you want to rent one, they offer that service as well. Otherwise the metal would just be sitting there. May as well make it work, moving the metal in more ways than one.'

'OK. Carry on.'

'Well, sitting there at night, listening to Radio Luxembourg, it dawned on me I could make more money by screwing the place.'

'Heard that before.' Yellich sipped his tea.

'So, took a stroll round, couldn't steal a motor . . . too noticeable and I can't drive anyway.'

'Now that would be an obstacle, I mean if you wanted to be a car thief.'

Michael Henderson grinned. 'Aye . . . but if they don't pay, it's tempting to screw them – any employer that doesn't pay is likely to get screwed by his workers. So I experimented, went out and set off the alarm of a car, nobody came, too remote; scared the badgers and the foxes and the owls, but that's all. Just walk up to a car, nudge it and the alarm goes off and sounds for about five minutes. Once had the alarm of all the cars going at once and me standing there waving my arms like I was conducting an orchestra . . . and not a soul turned up.'

'No dogs?'

'No. The owner had a thing about dogs, what do you call it? A phobia, so I was told, so he chose a remote location and hired a night watchie and trusted to luck. Anyway these motors had good radios and stereos and such . . . tool kits, jacks . . . so I decided I would screw all the cars in there.'

'How did you intend to carry all of that away if you can't drive?'

'Had a bike.'

'You cycled to work and back?'

'No, I was driven there. I went to the dealers at five p.m., there was always one or two motors going back to the storage place, returned hires, cars that couldn't be left on the forecourt overnight, and they left me there. Then, I'd get taken back to York at nine a.m. with one of the cars that was going back to the showroom.'

'Long shift.'

'Seventeen hours, but I could get my head down if it was quiet, and anyway, how many night watchies do you know who get chauffeur driven to and from work in a Rolls Royce?'

'Not many.' Yellich had to concede that one.

'But I decided to screw the place and hide what I took in the ruin.'

'The ruin?'

'Old house in the bottom corner of the waste ground.'

'You call it the waste ground?'

'Well, it's a field . . . was then, probably a housing estate now, but not cultivated, just letting the grass grow tall, all round was well under the plough but not this bit. About as big as a football pitch. Anyway, could see the old house from the watchman's hut, reckoned I could hide the stuff there. Go back for it, with a mate, got a mate with a van, or maybe ask my mate to come and screw the premises with me, unload the gear in the Vale. I had contacts then. Thought I'd ask my mate first, because occasionally I saw light on in the old house, sort of torchlight, or paraffin lamps . . . and a car's headlights . . . not often, so if my mate couldn't help me, I'd take the chance of stashing the gear in the old house and coming back for it.'

'The old house is a ruin? Torchlight, paraffin lamps?'

'Ruin, aye.'

'OK.'

'So I stuck it through that summer, light nights and all, then waited till winter started to come on, then I jacked it in. Could see their disappointment, who were they going to get now, in this weather?' He shrugged his shoulders. 'Suited me, all part of the plan. So I went back one night, on me bike, cutting tools, and went round the back of the premises in the bushes, those evergreen things that grow tall quickly, lot of fuss about them.'

'Leylandii?'

'Them.' Michael Henderson sipped his coffee with a slurp. 'And I was just about to start cutting when I heard someone on the waste ground, so I turned and saw what I saw, as best I could. It was dark and raining, like I said.'

'So what did you see?'

'Well I checked they hadn't got a watchie, left the light on in the site hut but no one was in there, so I set to, to cut the wire . . . I mean, this was twenty years ago, you're not going to do me for it, not when it comes as part of the information?'

'Probably not,' Yellich said guardedly, 'but only probably. Prosecuting for a minor crime so long after the event

9

is repressive and the Crown Prosecution Service doesn't like doing it, but that's the only reason, technically.'

'OK, technically, I can live with.' Michael Henderson sipped his coffee, again with an annoying slurp, and again he shrugged his shoulders. 'Anyway those shrubs then were only five feet tall, up to here.' He touched his shoulder. 'I heard a sound in the waste ground behind me. I thought I'd been rumbled, I couldn't take the slammer, only smokes in the slammer, no beer, I need my beer.'

'Just carry on, please.'

'I seen this guy pulling this lassie across the field by her wrists, as though both wrists were tied together . . . see, the only time I ever got lifted the police put handcuffs on me in the front of me –' Michael Henderson put both hands together in front of him – 'and the custody sergeant got hold of the chain between the cuffs and led me to the cell. One night in custody, escaped with a fine, first offence, see . . . first offence the police knew about. But the girl was being led like that, pulled along, slipping, sliding.'

'It was a dark night. You saw that clearly?'

'Clearly enough. My eyes were used to the dark then and if it's really dark you can see more than if there's a little bit of light, light prevents your eyes getting used to the dark, you see.'

'Sounds like you have experience of the night.'

'I have to make ends meet.'

'Alright.' Yellich had long, long ago resigned himself to the fact that if the police ever got to know about fifty percent of whatever is happening they can count themselves fortunate.

'Girl was naked. She was a white girl, stood out against the dark, a black girl may not have stood out so, but she was pink, like you, like me. Sort of sliding about on the wet grass, making a whimpering sound but not struggling, not pulling against the guy.'

'You realize all this is going to be checked? If you are wasting our time—'

'I'm not. I'm telling you this because I don't want to live with it anymore.'

'Alright, just so you're clear about the fact that you can't come in here and make statements like this with impunity.'

Michael Henderson plunged his hand into his pocket and brought out a nylon wallet, red, grubby, torn, velcro coming loose. He opened it and took out a piece of cardboard. 'DSS signing-on card, got my name on it, got my address.'

Yellich checked them and took a note of the serial number.

'Bus pass.' Henderson dropped another card on the table. 'That's got my photo and my address, confirming it's me.'

'OK.' Yellich handed the item back to Henderson.

'I'm registered disabled.'

'I noticed,' Yellich said, 'Disability Benefit.'

'Sciatica.' Henderson said with a smile. 'Bad back, awful pain.'

'Really . . . you don't seem to be suffering.'

'Well, you get more money with Disability Benefit and the Social leave you alone, don't get called in to be told to take this job or have your benefit stopped.'

'Got it all worked out, haven't you? Disability Benefit *and* a way of making ends meet. But carry on.'

'So this guy was pulling the girl over the waste ground and then just shoves her into a hole, there must have been a hole ready dug, she just went in there. There was another guy following them, carrying two spades. The girl stood up in the hole, I saw her top, say from the waist up and the second guy just brings the spade down on her head. I can still hear the sound. Then he hands the other spade to the first guy and they both start shovelling soil into the hole. Then, when they'd finished, they just walked away, calm as you please, like two mates walking home from the pub, side by side . . . like it was all in a day's work.'

'You saw all that?'

'Clearly enough. I was quite close, see they came from the derelict house, they seemed to want to bury her as far from the house as possible, that meant they came near to Mallards.'

'Anyway, I reckon I was only about twenty feet away and that's close when you are watching someone murdered. Just kept still, just kept silent, too scared to breathe, all the while they were filling the hole in the ground. I just wanted to run but daren't . . . they'd have done me. Anyway, they finished and walked away, like I said, calm as you please. That scared me more than anything, they didn't run, no hurry, they didn't seem to feel guilty, and they seemed in it together.'

'As one, would you say?'

'Aye, that's a good way of putting it. As one.'

'Then?'

'I stayed in the shrubs, heard a car start up, somewhere near the old house, but later, not immediately . . . as though they were taking their time over something.'

'How much later?'

'Possibly an hour. It's a long time ago, but I remember I was scared by that too, scared by the calm way they walked away, scared by the fact that they had just murdered a lassie and didn't seem anxious to clear the pitch like I would have been. I mean if I had done that, I would have run.'

'And left lots of lovely clues behind you. But they were calm, as if picking up after themselves. Yes, I can see how you would be scared. Anything about the car you can recall? Petrol? Diesel?'

'Petrol . . . sounded small, not large, a bit tinny, nothing to stand out like a VW Beetle would have stood out by its sound – phut, phut, phut – nothing like that. After that I stayed there in the shrubs, till dawn came, reckoned it was safe to move then, so I moved. Cycled back to York, got back to York as the rush hour was beginning, looked just like a regular workie going to his job, but I was shaking like a leaf inside. I'd just seen a woman killed. I was too scared to go back the next night to get the hi-fis, I mean, knowing what was in the clay.'

'I imagine you found other ways of making ends meet. Tell me about the two guys. Large? Small? Young? Old?'

'Young I'd say, twenties . . . one was more overweight than the other, one was slim . . .' His voice trailed off, he paled and looked unwell.

'Mr Henderson?'

'There were two more . . . I thought I'd remembered it all, but there were two more, two more came after. It's the way you remember. You think you've remembered it all, then something else comes to mind . . . Oh, my . . .'

'There were four? Four guys?'

'No . . . the other two were different, those two guys were tall, muscular, the other two were short. I think one was a lassie. Do you have a smoke?' Yellich fished into his pocket and brought out a packet of nails. Michael Henderson grabbed for one with short, stubby, grubby fingers and held it in his mouth while Yellich flicked a slender disposable lighter to produce a modest flame.

'You don't smoke yourself?'

'No,' Yellich smiled. 'These are just props, things to help an interview along.'

'Well, you're a young man, keep off them.'

'I intend to.' Yellich relaxed back in his chair. 'So now we have a gang of four?'

'The other two came as I was wondering whether it was safe to leave. They came silently, two short figures, two men I thought 'cos the lassie walked like a guy, but she turned side on and I saw her profile . . . she had breasts . . . it was a lassie; short and a bit fat. The guy was small, really small. They just came and stood over the grave, where the girl had been put, just stood there, not saying anything, and then turned away without a word being spoken, as though they knew what each other was thinking. I remember now, that's why I stayed until dawn. I was about to move, I realized I could've run into them, so I was scared to move after that. It was after they had walked away that I heard the car start. Then I waited till dawn. Then I moved.' Michael Henderson paused again.

'You've remembered something else?' Yellich raised his eyebrow, a futile gesture because Henderson's head was buried into his fleshy paws.

'Aye . . . the lad, the short guy, he dropped something on the ground, on the grave, something white. I heard it thud. Like a rock or something. It was as if they were marking the grave.'

'And the lassie they murdered? How old would you say?'

'Young . . . twenties, very young . . . nice looking girl that I could see, thin . . . good figure . . . then the next day or the next, or the one after that, it all just went from my mind and it all stayed buried until one night a few months ago, when I was in the tap room of the Green Man.'

'And now you are here.'

'And now I'm here, at least I came, later, better than never.'

'Alright. Let's get this down in the form of a statement, then you and I are going to take a drive.'

'We are?'

'We are. We're going back there. And later today, if you recall anything at all, no matter how trivial . . .'

'Don't worry, I'll be here like a shot. Best thing I ever did. I feel better in myself.'

'You'd've felt better if you had phoned us at the time, even anonymously. That girl would have had a family. That's twenty years of anguish for someone . . . parents if they're still alive, brothers, sisters.'

'It just went from my mind, automatically like. I didn't deliberately block it out. And I came as soon as I remembered it, give or take a few months . . .'

'Alright.' Yellich picked up his pen. 'Let's see what we can rescue from this, but after twenty years, all we're likely to get is a body for some poor soul to lay to rest in a more appropriate hole.'

Forty-five minutes later Yellich escorted Michael Henderson to the public area in front of the enquiry desk and asked him to take a seat, and once again Michael Henderson sat on the wood-hard surface of a bench which appeared to be soft and inviting. Yellich returned to his desk and picked up the phone and jabbed a four figure internal number.

'Collator!' The voice was crisp, eager, youthful sounding, female.

'DS Yellich.'

'Yes, sir?'

'Missing persons.'

'Yes, sir . . . ?'

'Female, possibly in her twenties, disappeared about

15

twenty years ago, possibly reported missing from the York area.'

'Very good, sir, about twenty years ago?'

'Sorry to be so vague. Can you look over a ten-year time window, say from fifteen to twenty-five years ago?'

'Can do. Information to you, sir?'

'Yes, or DCI Hennessey if I am not in the station.'

'Very good, sir.'

Yellich replaced the phone and walked back to the enquiry desk, he placed the statement taken from Michael Henderson in Hennessey's pigeonhole and added a post-script to the effect that the collator had been contacted. He signed out 'to the crime scene', lifted the hinged section of the desk, walked into the public area and stood in front of Michael Henderson. 'Okay,' he said, 'let's take a trip down "Memory Lane".'

The location was as Henderson had described, remote. He directed Yellich to an obscure left turn off the main York to Selby Road which they followed for perhaps half a mile, going deeper and deeper into the countryside, and with the occasional leaf falling, caught in the wind and blown across the front of the vehicle. It was not by any means the great deluge of leaves that would fall in a matter of weeks' time, but nonetheless, autumn was in the air.

'Here.' Henderson nodded to the left, at another obscure turn, narrower than the first, and this led for a few hundred yards to a derelict house. Just before the house, the road turned to the right and went towards a stand of Leylandii which stood like a line of infantry and about twenty feet tall.

'They've grown,' Henderson said.

'They tend to.' Yellich halted the car. 'That's why there's so much fuss about them. Damn eyesore if you ask me, and most of them are underground, massive root system that steals water and nutrients from other plants, that's also why there's a big fuss about them.'

'Well, this is it. And not built on.'

Yellich switched the engine off. The area was, he would have to concede, more or less just as Henderson had described it to be. In front of where he had parked the car was a derelict building, a small house it seemed, clearly of an earlier era, much earlier. So derelict that a tree had managed to find its way from the soil beneath the house through a hole in the roof. Very derelict. To the far right was the stand of Leylandii, behind which was a parking/storage space for motor cars for Mallard & Co, 'Purveyors and Hirers of the finest automobiles', as Yellich recalled their slogan to be, and between the derelict house and the Leylandii and stretched back until it reached a woodland was a generous parcel of land, about, as Henderson had said, as large as a football pitch, and as he had also said, strangely uncultivated or developed. Just lying fallow, allowing coarse grass to dominate it.

'OK.' Yellich switched off the engine. 'From here we walk.'

'Could get closer if you go down Mallards Lane, they won't use it at this time of day, it's still forenoon.' Yellich warmed to Henderson's use of an outmoded expression. But he was insistent. 'We walk. It'll do you good.' He got out of the car, a grumbling Michael Henderson did likewise.

It was, thought Yellich, a good walking day. Dry, not too cold, not unbearably hot either, a day for a pullover and a coat or jacket. The tops of the Leylandii swayed gently and the sky was of a uniform grey, a low cloud base, but rain was not threatened. A gentle five-minute stroll took Yellich and Henderson to the Leylandii, and the entrance to Mallard's. They climbed from the road to the waste ground and walked alongside the perimeter of the trees, and then turned to their right as the trees turned in their square formation, and walked on for a few paces until Henderson said, 'It was about here.'

'About?'

Without a reply, Henderson pushed his way between two Leylandii and Yellich heard him stumbling in the undergrowth, and then in a gesture that Yellich would have found comic had the circumstances not been so tragic, Henderson burst from the Leylandii a few feet further along them with a look of undisguised triumph and said, 'No. Here.'

Yellich joined him. 'Sure?'

'Sure. I know where I was in relation to the watchman's hut. It's still there, still in the same place.'

'Alright. So you said you were about twenty feet away?'

'About. I've been accurate so far.' Henderson glanced out across the field of coarse grass. 'Part of me wishes it was a dream, but it's looking like it wasn't.'

'I can understand that. So, which direction?'

'That way.' Henderson extended an arm describing an angle of about forty-five degrees from the line of trees.

'About twenty feet?' Yellich despaired as he pondered the coarse grass. The prospect of finding undisturbed soil after that length of time was zero. It was a job for ground radar, and with the police budget being what it was, the prospect of obtaining use for it on the basis of the uncorroborated statement of a drunk about an incident which may or may not have happened twenty-plus years ago . . . It was, thought Yellich, hardly worth putting in the requisition. His only hope was in locating the white object which Henderson claimed he saw dropped, as if the grave was being marked. He walked forwards, brushing the grass away from him as he did so.

The object Henderson had seen contemptuously tossed on to a shallow grave revealed itself to be a house brick, an ordinary house brick, painted white, or whitewashed. After twenty years the paint or whitewash was much faded but it was there, having been preserved from the glare of the sun in summer, and the slicing winds of the winter, by the coarse grass in which it lay. And further, astoundingly, it lay about twenty feet from where Henderson had remained standing by the tree line. And it had clearly been there for a very long time: about twenty years. Twenty feet, twenty years. The last suspicion about the accuracy of Henderson's recovered memory evaporated from Yellich's mind as he became certain that he stood near a shallow grave and that a murder inquiry was about to be launched. He and Yellich walked back to the car in silence.

'I'll enjoy my beer,' Henderson said, suddenly, as a skein of geese flew overhead, just beneath the cloud base, heading south.

'What?' Yellich turned to him, ruddy faced, ambling along, looking pleased with himself.

'My beer, I'll enjoy it tonight. I haven't for the last few months, but I'll enjoy it tonight. Pressure's off me, see, it's off me.'

'Lucky you.' Yellich turned and looked at the derelict house. But he knew what Henderson meant. Henderson had done his part, his part in the scheme of this thing was over, behind him. Yellich's part was to come. They reached the car and Henderson, uninvited, got in. Yellich opened the driver's door and reached for the radio microphone, then remembering its unreliability and tendency of its signal to breaking up, he replaced it and took out his mobile. He dialled Micklegate Bar Police Station and asked to speak to Detective Chief Inspector Hennessey.

'Yellich, sir.' He said when Hennessey answered.

'Yellich, I've read your submission. Does it have substance, you think?'

'Appears to, sir. Everything is as Mr Henderson reported. I have even found a white-painted brick in the grass.'

'As if marking the grave, so the murderers can revisit the exact spot, as is said that they do.'

'As if indeed, sir. I think we have to consider this a crime scene.'

'Right. I'll join you. Scenes of Crime Unit, constables with spades, anything else?'

'Just a car to convey Mr Henderson back to York, sir. If he could be dropped near a pub, any pub, I think he'll be happy with that.' He glanced at his watch: getting on for midday. 'They'll have been open for an hour by the time he gets back.'

'Extra car. Have you had your refreshment?'

'Nothing since breakfast, sir.'

'I'll bring you a sandwich from the canteen.'

'I'd appreciate it, sir.'

MONDAY, 12.00–13.30 HRS

George Hennessey followed Yellich's directions and arrived at the scene. He was accompanied by a van containing six constables and a sergeant, and a single constable driving a police vehicle, this last coming only to pick up Michael Henderson so as to convey him to York. The van containing the Scenes of Crime Officer arrived shortly after Michael Henderson had been driven away from the scene.

'All here.' Hennessey's silver hair was tugged gently in the breeze. 'Lead on, Yellich.'

Yellich led on and took the assembled company down the road leading towards Mallard's, hidden behind the softly swaying Leylandii, on to the waste land and to where the brick, covered with fading white paint or whitewash, lay. The constables, each carrying a spade, looked to Yellich to be solemn faced, as well, he thought, they might. It was not the prospect of discovering a body that daunted them, that was well in all their strides, but the backbreaking work of digging soil that had not, allegedly, been turned for twenty years. Having established the location, Yellich nodded to the sergeant. 'All yours, sergeant.' He picked up the brick and stepped backwards.

'Right, lads.' The sergeant spoke with false humour. 'Could be worse . . . could be the depths of winter and rock-hard soil, could be the height of summer, but it's not, nice cool, early autumn day, just the right sort of day for a spot of gardening . . . OK, get sweating.'

The six constables, arranged in a generous circle, began to attack the soil around where the white brick had lain, the brick having by then been placed in a production bag and tagged.

'The house is part of it?' Hennessey looked at the ruin.

'It appears to have been, sir. The informant told of lights burning therein and of the people involved coming from the direction of the house . . . of cars being parked there rather than nearer the grave as one might have expected.'

'Shall we take a look? It'll take some time to excavate the grave.' Hennessey and Yellich walked to the ruin, in silence. They halted in front of it.

'Date?'

21

'September 22nd, sir, or 23rd.'

'Of the house, Yellich.'

'Oh, wouldn't know, sir, sorry. I thought military history was your passion, not architecture.'

'It spills over. History is a vast place and you focus but you also find yourself diverging. It's a curious building.'

'Small, boss.'

'It's a gatehouse, remnant of an estate. There's a similar one in Leeds, nicely renovated, and looking very homely, a little bit of eighteenth century surrounded by 1930s semis. This is eighteenth century too.'

'Oh, yes, 1765.'

'How can you tell?'

'It says so . . . above the door.'

'Ah . . . yes . . . I was doing it the hard way, didn't notice the date. We can expect to find curved doors inside.'

'Curved doors?'

'They were fashionable in the latter half of the eighteenth century, steam power having been harnessed. They found that if you expose wood to steam it becomes pliable and it can be bent, and if you clamp it on to a last it solidifies in the curved position. Anyway, let's see what we see, careful how you go . . . it looks unsafe . . . the stonework seems solid but the timbers will be rotten.'

Hennessey stepped into the house. Yellich followed. Hennessey tested the floorboards gingerly before entrusting them with his full weight.

'No cellar,' he observed, 'unusual that.'

Yellich followed his gaze through a large hole in the floorboards. Vegetation grew about ten inches below their feet. 'Not far to fall if the floorboards do give way.'

'Not on the ground floor anyway, but we'll go upstairs

if we can. Keep to the edge of the room, the floor will be strongest there.'

Hennessey and Yellich walked gingerly round the ground floor of the house; it was as both officers expected, windowless, covered with bird droppings, rotten timber which nonetheless revealed a high level of carpentry. Yellich pondered his old woodwork teacher 'Pecker' as in 'woodpecker', who on principle never gave more than $9\frac{1}{2}$ out of 10 on the basis that nothing can be perfect, but these joints, he thought, would get full marks even from grumpy 'Pecker'. And they were nearly two hundred and fifty years old. Two hundred and fifty years ago English craftsmen had mastered carpentry to that level. But the officers saw nothing which appeared to be relevant to the inquiry.

'Let's risk the stairs.' Hennessey led the way, stepping gingerly on each step at its very edge, and with Yellich following, ascended to the first floor, or what remained of the first floor, for the tree had pushed up through the rotting floorboards and out of the roof. Again, it was windowless, again bird droppings littered what remained of the floor. But one room, just one room, chilled the officers. It was a small room, the sort of room that would in later years be called a box room, perhaps ten feet by ten feet; it too had no glass in the window frame, the floor of the room too was covered with bird droppings, but this room had a fixture which was not part of the original design. There was an eye bolt in the skirting board. A length of heavy chain about four feet long was attached to the eye bolt. A padlock was fastened to the chain, six links from the end. The officers looked at it in silence and then Yellich knelt and took the end of the chain and held the last link to the padlock, thus creating a loop.

'Just the circumference to fit round a human ankle,' said Hennessey. 'Or a human wrist.'

'Here.' Yellich extended his finger to the skirting board. 'Six notches have been cut into it at intervals. Too wide for a knife.'

'Try the chain.'

Yellich took the chain and placed a link against one of the notches. 'Perfect fit,' he said. 'Tells a story. Someone used the chain to score a notch in the skirting board, Robinson Crusoe-like. What do you think, boss? One notch for every day?'

'Has to be.' Hennessey stepped back from the doorway. 'Better leave that as we found it for the SOCO to photograph, then we'll recover it for bagging and tagging.'

Yellich stood. 'This is shaping up to be something nasty, boss.'

Hennessey and Yellich returned to the excavation. The constables, he noted, had by then dug a wide hole, which, by then, was approximately two feet deep.

'Nothing so far, gentlemen,' the sergeant said. 'Nothing at all, just soil. Could do with some of this for the garden, it's lovely and rich.'

'As well it ought to be,' Yellich said. 'Hasn't grown anything for a very long time, nothing's been taken out of it, except what the grass takes. Hasn't supported crops at all. But keep at it, the witness reports the victim to have been waist deep in the hole . . . at least another foot to go. If you don't come across anything when you are four feet down . . .' Yellich glanced at Hennessey, who nodded. 'If you don't find anything when you are four feet down, we'll leave it at that, but somehow, I think you'll find something.'

Half an hour later they did.

It was Monday, 13.30 hours.

Two

. . . in which a corpse is looked in the mouth,
and a police officer's wife remembers an obscure
word which neatly sums up the situation.

MONDAY, 14.30–22.30 HRS

The skeleton had first appeared to human view as a
white stone, about the size of a large coin of the
realm, whereupon a youthful constable – perhaps, guessed
Hennessey, the least experienced of the six – had by
judgement or intuition stopped driving his spade into the
loam and said, 'Hold it!' The other five had held it as
the sixth used the spade delicately to scrape away soil
inch by inch and the white stone became larger, rounder,
became a skull, a human skull. The digging then became
more focused and more gentle, gradually revealing a full
human skeleton, still with the wrists bound in front. It
was all exactly as Michael Henderson had recalled.

At the discovery of the skeleton, before it was fully
revealed, Hennessey asked Yellich to use his 'brain fryer'
to ask for the attendance of the forensic pathologist at the
scene. Yellich had done so and almost coincidentally,
with the last small amount of soil being scraped from
the feet of the skeleton, Hennessey's eye was caught by
a motor car halting near the police vehicle, still parked
by the derelict house. The car was a distinctive red and
white Riley, circa 1947. Hennessey gave no outward sign

of emotion but he smiled inwardly and felt a warmth of emotion as he watched the driver get out of the vehicle. The car had rear-hinging doors, frowned upon in the safety-conscious early twenty-first century, but in the middle of the previous century the danger of the doors was unforeseen or was suppressed to allow the convenience of the design. The driver swivelled neatly in the seat, put out both legs together, in a ladylike manner, although she was wearing green coveralls. She stood and looked briefly at the group of officers as if acknowledging their presence, then turned and reached back inside the car and extracted a black bag. She closed the car door, did not, noted Hennessey, feel the need to lock it, and began to walk towards the activity on the waste ground. She was slender. Underneath the white cap she wore, Hennessey knew she had very close-cropped, dark hair, greying slightly. She was a lady who was allowing herself to grow old gracefully. He noted the time of the arrival of the forensic pathologist in his notebook for his later report. It was 14.30 precisely, though he wrote 14.31 so as to give the impression of accuracy. 14.30, whilst truthful, would, he thought, give an impression of approximation. So 14.31 it was.

Louise D'Acre walked in her own time to the group of officers, the uniformed officers by then having withdrawn to a reverential distance, leaving Hennessey and Yellich to stand sentinel beside the grave.

'Dr D'Acre.' Hennessey doffed his hat when Louise D'Acre reached his personal space.

'Chief Inspector.' Louise D'Acre nodded but gave no hint of emotion. She was, as Hennessey had always found her to be, focused, practical, single-mindedly addressing the task in question. 'Ah . . .' She glanced into the shallow grave. 'Confess I did wonder why the usual intelligence about the police surgeon confirming life extinct was not conveyed.'

'Not required in the event of skeletal remains being discovered.' Hennessey quoted from police standing orders.

'Female –' Louise D'Acre pondered the skeleton – 'compressed fracture of the rear of the skull, I can tell that from here. Heavy, flat object delivered with some force caused that injury, which in itself would be fatal.'

'Our witness described a spade.'

'Witness!' Louise D'Acre turned to Hennessey with clear surprise. 'But the body has been there for years. The flesh has completely disappeared, the major organs too . . . that doesn't happen in a weekend, not even a bank holiday weekend.'

'We think she was murdered about twenty years ago.' Hennessey then related the story of Michael Henderson's statement.

'Sounds like more of a confession than a statement.' Louise D'Acre once again pondered the skeleton. 'But a spade would do nicely, just the job, flatten the back of the head like that, just the tool for the job. Wrists seem to be fastened together. Is that a chain I see?'

'It is, so we believe. We haven't been down to examine it but that is consistent with our witness's statement.'

'Well, let's take a look. Have you taken all the snapshots you want to take?' Dr D'Acre snapped on a pair of latex gloves.

Hennessey glanced at Yellich. 'All taken, sir, from every angle.'

'OK then.' Dr D'Acre turned and stepped backwards into the shallow pit, the last resting place of one human of the female sex, identity to be determined. Dr D'Acre knelt by the skeleton and examined its length, standing over it, peering at it, but clearly making sure she didn't stand on the bones. 'I can detect no other injuries,' she said. Though Hennessey was unsure whether this was for her own edification or for his. He remained silent, judging it to be the more prudent option. 'If in doubt, say nowt.' He reflected on the ancient gem of Yorkshire wisdom, and said 'nowt'.

Louise D'Acre stood. 'That's all I can do here, gentlemen. If you could have the skeleton lifted out, I'll address the post-mortem as soon as it arrives at York District Hospital.' She levered herself out of the hole with subtle athleticism. Few women in their forties, thought Hennessey, could manage such a feat. Yellich too was not unimpressed by the good doctor's evident strength and dexterity.

'What do you know of the murder?' D'Acre brushed her hands, one against the other to remove the soil, then peeled off the gloves.

'We believe she was kept in that house for a while and brought here in the night.'

'For a period of time?'

Hennessey told D'Acre about the grooves which appeared to have been scored in the skirting board and of the chain that appeared to have been used to effect said scoring.

'May I see?' D'Acre asked. 'It is of course of no relevance to the PM and will add nothing to my findings, but I'd like to see it.'

Hennessey walked with Dr D'Acre to the derelict house, whilst Yellich supervised the lifting of the skeleton on to the stretcher, and its placement inside a body bag, and the further placement of the body bag inside the mortuary van which had been brought up and parked close to the excavation.

Louise D'Acre viewed the small room, she saw the

grooves carved into the skirting board. 'Have you ever had a supernatural experience?' she asked of Hennessey.

'Well . . . yes . . . you know I have.'

'I'm sorry, that was insensitive of me . . . but do you have any feelings about this house?'

'I don't . . . just a crumbling ruin of a building.'

'Something evil happened in this house. I can sense it . . . I am not usually given to entertaining the para-normal but I can feel something here, that's why there's no graffiti on the walls, it isn't because the house is too remote to be a den for the local youth, it's because there is an atmosphere here. Children could sense it and I tell you a dog wouldn't come in here.' Louise D'Acre glanced out of the window at the expanse of wasteland. 'How many more, do you think?'

'More?'

'Yes, more. Buried out there after spending their last days in here enduring heaven knows what torture and torment. I mean the young female out there, because it is a young skeleton, the young female out there is not necessarily the earthly remains of the desperate person-ality who etched a record of her last days in the skirting board. So what do you think? Two, twenty . . . ?'

But George Hennessey didn't hear Louise D'Acre's last words, inside he was reeling with the implication of her observation as a chill shot down his spine and his scalp crawled. She was, he conceded, probably correct. The wasteland must be assumed to hold other dark secrets.

Hennessey and Yellich returned to Micklegate Bar Police Station, signed in and walked down the echoing CID corridor to their respective offices. Hennessey took off his coat and hat, hung them on the stand by the small window and, as he did so, glanced across Nunnery Lane to the walls, where a group of Japanese tourists walked the battlements, thrilling, it seemed, to the antiquity. The air was then pierced by a shrill whistle; a locomotive was being steamed up in the Railway Museum. He plugged in the electric kettle that stood on the table by the window, after testing its weight to ensure there was sufficient water inside, poured coffee granules into the bottom of a mug, added milk taken from his mini fridge. While he waited for the kettle to boil, he crossed to his desk and punched a four-figure internal number.

'Collator.'

'DCI Hennessey. DS Yellich sent a request earlier today?'

'Yes, sir, have the results here for you. We accessed four files from the archives, just arrived now in fact, no time yet to have put a note about them in your pigeonhole.'

'Very good. Have them sent up to me please.'

'Very good, sir. On their way.'

'Thank you.' Hennessey replaced the phone, returned to the kettle, waited for it to steam, holding it by the handle, and as he did so, he once again noticed his heavily liver-spotted hand. Just a few more years, then retirement, long in coming, hard in the earning. Mug of coffee in hand, he returned to his desk, sat in his chair, waiting for the liquid to cool, waiting for the files to be brought by the collator.

They were brought to him by an eager looking, fresh-faced cadet, who to Hennessey looked too young to be a police cadet. She was, he thought, the sort of girl who would not look out of place in the starched shirt and pleated skirt of a school uniform. Liver spots and cadets who didn't just look young, but who looked too young: his retirement, still a year or two off, was clearly highly appropriate.

'Files, sir,' she said, handing them to Hennessey. 'I was asked to bring them to you, sir.'

'Thank you.' Hennessey took them from the girl. 'New here?'

'Yes, sir. This is my first week.'

'You are?'

'Tracy Whitlock, sir.'

'Welcome aboard, Tracy, and thank you again for them.'

'Thank you, sir.' Tracy Whitlock blushed and left the room.

Hennessey put the files on his desk, turned them the right way round and thought how in less than five years the enthusiastic, eager-to-please, thrilled-in-the-new-job-and-uniform Tracy Whitlock would have been turned into a harder, more cynical WPC Whitlock. It is the nature of police work.

Sipping the coffee, he scanned the four files, taking notes as he did so. They could, and doubtless would, be trawled for details later. At that early stage he wanted a quick overview and was dismayed with what he found. Half an hour after beginning to read the first file, he looked no further at the files – they were too cluttered, too difficult to access, the nuts and bolts of the situation had been conveyed to his notepad: in the space of eight years, four young women had been reported missing, all from the Holgate area of York, that part of York that the tourists don't visit, blackened terraced houses, small corner shops, struggling pubs, where washing is strung across the street, where unemployment is high. The area of bedsits of the 'night people' of the city and the area where students find alternative accommodation to that offered by the university. And there lay the first clue as to how such a tragedy could be allowed to unfold, because all the missing persons had been undergraduates at the time of their disappearance. They were:

> Joyce Bush of 10 Don Grove, Holgate, YO26,
>   aged 20
> Melita Campion of 9 Wharfe Terrace, Holgate,
>   YO26, aged 19
> Charlotte Philips of 27 Aire Road, Holgate,
>   YO26, aged 21
> Christine Tate of 2 Ribble Road, Holgate,
>   YO26, aged 20

Their home addresses varied – Joyce Bush's home address was given as being in Bristol, Melita Campion was a London girl from Greenwich, Charlotte Philips was more local, from Derbyshire, and Christine Tate was a Liverpudlian. They had been attending different establishments in York, one at the university, another at the School of Drama and so on. The time span between the first reported disappearance and the last, between Joyce Bush and Christine Tate, was a period of eight years, nine months. The first reported of the four disappearances was nearly thirty years ago. They had all been part of the transient population, not missed by the settled community of YO26 because students keep shops and pubs in business but don't engage with 'the locals' and so would not have been missed as local girls would have been, and moreover, would not have had their disappearances linked as would the disappearances of local girls. The 'mis per' cases were each handled by different police officers, and all had been perfunctory – statements taken, recent photographs acquired and that was it, nothing to do until the person or the corpse turned up, either in suspicious or non-suspicious circumstances.

That is just the way of it. It is now, it was then, and George Hennessey was convinced that it would continue to be the way of it. Searches of local areas, likely haunts, can be made for very young children who go missing, often with an army of volunteers, occasionally indeed, with the aid of the army itself, but anybody over the age of fifteen is searched for only by frantic relatives or devoted friends. They turn up alive with a story to tell, or deceased, their bodies having another story to tell. Only then, if appropriate, do the police become involved. It cannot in all practicality and with stretched resources be any other way. And so all the files, representing as they did, the grief and desperation of families who by now must have accepted the inevitable, but wanted to know, just to know what had happened to their daughter/sister, and hopefully, hopefully, to have a body to bury, were slender files in the extreme. Each photograph was of a young, happy-looking woman with a toothpaste advert for a smile, each clearly loving life, each happy to be alive, yet each photograph was 'recent'. Within weeks of having their joyful likeness captured for posterity, in a frame on a relative's mantelpiece, each of the young women would have been deceased. And no one had made the link. Over a period of eight years, four different detectives would not have linked each other's investigations, the student community would have known only about individual disappearances, not all four. Even then there may still have been no link at all, each young woman might have met her death by misadventure, their bodies still waiting to be discovered, or they may simply have taken new identities to escape a poisonous home life. The only thing in fact which did link them was the cluster of their last known addresses, that series of terraced housing in YO26, where all the streets are named after a local river, and known, not surprisingly, as 'the rivers'. Further, they all might continue to be 'mis pers'; the skeleton that Hennessey knew was by then on a stainless-steel table in the pathology laboratory of York District Hospital, might not be that of Joyce, Melita, Charlotte or Christine.

'The corpse is that of a female and is skeletal.' Dr D'Acre spoke for the benefit of a microphone which was attached to a stainless-steel anglepoise arm which was suspended from the ceiling, directly above the dissecting table. 'That the remains are those of an adult of the female sex is determined by the skull, being of the rounder, smoother appearance, rather than the more rugged male skull. The skull is also smaller in overall size than would be the case if it was that of a male. The muscle ridges of the skull are not as marked as they would have been had this been a male skull, the orbits are set higher on the face than if it had been a male skull, and the forehead is high and steep. The deceased is clearly an adult, therefore post-pubertal, and the pelvis is wider and more shallow than the male counterpart. The sacrum is noted to be wide with a shallow curve, again indicating that this skeleton is of the female sex. The femur is longer than I would have expected it to be if these were the remains of a person of the male sex. So, a female –' Dr D'Acre turned to Yellich – 'as your witness described.'

'Indeed.' It was the only thing he could think of to say. It sounded to him to be quite weak. He added, 'How old d'you think she was?'

'All in good time, Sergeant. All in good time.'

'In respect of her race, she appears to have been north-western European or Caucasian. The skull is high and long, the sagittal contour is rounded, the nasal opening is narrow, the orbital opening is angular, the lower nasal margin is sharp and the nasal profile is straight. A white European. You ask her age? Well, the appearance is that of a young woman, no signs of any degenerative disease, like arthritis in the bones, no sign of healed fractures caused by previous injuries sustained in an earlier phase of life, no pubic scarring – she hadn't given birth. But the real information will be in the mouth, an Aladdin's cave of information. She is believed to have been murdered about twenty years ago, you say?'

'About that, yes.'

'Well, that may cause problems in identifying her; it depends on the length of time her dentist keeps his records. Dentists are legally obliged to keep records for eleven years, thereafter they may dispose of them. If her dentist had a clear-out . . . identification may be a problem. It may have to be done by superimposing a photograph of her in life over a photograph of the skull, which will determine her identity if the orbits of the skull accommodate her eyes in the photograph and her face is accommodated by the size of the skull. You know the technique?'

'I do, yes.'

'Or the face could be reconstructed, and a very near-likeness achieved.'

'So I have noticed in other cases.'

'But that's really your department. I can only tell you how she died, but we'll come to that in a moment.' Dr D'Acre took a long stainless-steel rod and forced it between the skeleton's mouth; she levered the rod and the mouth opened with a loud 'crack'. She stepped back and then stood closer to the skeleton, peering into the mouth. 'There's something in here . . . something alien.'

'There is?'

'There is. Have you got a production bag?'

'I haven't.'

'Mr Filey . . . can we have a small production bag, please.' Dr D'Acre turned to Yellich with a smile. 'Let you have one of ours.' Mr Filey left the pathology laboratory. Yellich had met Filey before, and always found him to be warm and jovial, unlike any other mortuary attendant he had met. As a breed of men, they had always seemed to Yellich to be humourless individuals, either made that way by the nature of their job, or drawn to the job because that is their nature: chicken and egg. But Filey was a man apart. Yellich could see him running a small shop, giving sweets as treats to the children, but only in their parents' presence. Yellich thought him that sort of man.

'This young woman was leaving you a present.' Dr D'Acre's comments brought Yellich's mind back to the matter in hand, as the short, rotund Mr Filey returned with a handful of production bags. Yellich liked him for that as well, a man going the second mile. He handed a bag to Dr D'Acre who mumbled a 'thank you' as she took it. She held it in one hand and with a pair of tweezers extracted something from the mouth of the skeleton, something which Yellich thought looked like a small bundle. Dr D'Acre dropped the item into the production bag and sealed it. 'Did your witness say this girl was shaking or screaming or pleading for her life when he watched her being murdered?'

'No . . .' Yellich spoke softly, 'he said she was silent, as if resigned to her fate, or because there was no one to hear her shouting anyway.'

'Well, she may have been resigned but the reason she was silent was because she held this in her mouth.' She held up the production bag as Yellich approached her. 'It's a small pen, a small ballpoint, inside a cellophane bag.'

'It's a bookie's pen,' Yellich said. 'People who work in betting shops use them. Why they opt for very small pens, I don't know, but that's what it is.'

'Courageous girl.' Dr D'Acre handed the bag to Yellich. 'She knew she was going to be murdered, probably didn't know about the shallow grave, hoped her body might be found sooner rather than later, and she took this with her. The only reason she would do that was to leave some clue as to the identity of her murderers. There appears to be some writing on the pen; can't make it out, but the plastic has preserved it sufficiently for it to be made out in laboratory conditions . . . even a low-powered microscope would do the trick.'

'I'll log it and have it sent to the forensic laboratory at Wetherby. It could be quite a breakthrough.'

'Oh, I think it will be.' Dr D'Acre turned to the skeleton. 'Evidence of dental work . . . a couple of fillings, teeth were in good shape but fillings mean there were at one time dental records. I'll extract a tooth from the upper set of teeth, saw that in half and that will give her age to within twelve months, age at time of death, that is. That information will be with my report. I'll amputate the jaw and keep that aside. The lower teeth can be matched with the dental records, if they are still available, that's where the fillings are anyway. Right, so we know what sex she is, what race she is, we have received a gift she left for us, we will soon find her age and from her lower teeth, her identity, if we are lucky. Now let us turn to the crime, for crime it is. The wrists are fastened together at the anterior of the body by a thin chain and two small padlocks. Doubt if there's anything there to help you, Sergeant – you can get that stuff from any hardware shop. In fact, I bought just such a length of chain and put just such a padlock to secure the gate at the side of my house. I can't get the chain off without cutting it, even in this skeletal state the hand is still too wide to allow the chain to be pulled over it, it was probably fastened quite tightly round the wrist. Mr Filey . . .'

'Yes, Doctor?'

'A saw please. If I hold the chain against the table . . .'

Filey took a small hacksaw from a drawer and proceeded to cut the chain round one wrist while Dr D'Acre held it as tautly as she could. It seemed to Yellich that he sawed through the chain quite easily; he commented so.

'The length of time in the ground will have reduced the metal's integrity,' Dr D'Acre said. 'It would not cut as easily as this if it were new.' Filey then sawed through the chain around the other wrist and, without being asked, put the length of chain, plus the two padlocks, in a production bag, which he then handed to Yellich with a deferential nod and a smile.

'So, she was restrained at the time of death, at least partially so. Her feet were not fastened together, which would have been much more disabling. But to continue, a depressed fracture of the skull is noted, appears to have been caused by a single massive blow with a heavy, flat object, which I find to be utterly consistent with the reported statement that she was struck on the head with the blade of a spade. Death would have been instantaneous. No soil was found in the mouth or the nasal cavity. She was dead when they covered up her body . . .' Dr D'Acre paused, 'and twenty years later, you have returned to tell your tale and give us a little something to help us. You would have been a woman in your forties now, husband, grown-up children . . . but . . .' Dr D'Acre drummed her fingers on the dissecting table, 'but that will be the conclusion of my report, Sergeant: death was caused by major trauma to the skull. In life she was a young woman of Caucasian extraction. Exact age to be determined. I'll fax my report to Chief Inspector Hennessey as soon as it has been word processed. Tomorrow at the earliest.'

George Hennessey had, with a troubled mind, taken the four missing persons files to Commander Sharkey and appraised him of the events of that day.

'A bumbling drunk has opened a real can of worms.' Sharkey was a man who was small for a police officer, and at forty-five, young to be a commander. Very young. Framed photographs of him in the uniform of a lieutenant in the British Army and of him in the uniform of an officer of the Royal Hong Kong Police Force told the route by which he had arrived at his present position.

'It seems so, sir.' Hennessey leaned forward in the chair in which he sat in front of Sharkey's 'everything in its place' desk. 'Along with a comment by Dr D'Acre . . . and just looking at the land. If one of these four has been buried there, then the others may be there too.'

'You're not proposing to dig up the whole area?'

'No, sir. The white painted brick was clearly placed as a marker. Looks innocent enough unless you knew its significance and it's not the sort of thing that anyone would pick up and remove. Murderers like to revisit the scene of their crime . . . the brick was a marker to enable the murderers to do that. I'd like to muster a squad of officers to walk across the area of wasteland. Twenty should do it, shoulder to shoulder. If we divide the area into strips, each strip to accommodate said twenty officers walking in a line, we ought to find other house bricks. If, and it's a big if, the skeleton we exhumed this afternoon is one of these four missing women, and if the murderers used the same method of marking each shallow grave . . .'

'Big if as you say, George –' Sharkey raised an eyebrow, then added – 'two very big ifs in fact, but I think you are right. We have to walk the area. Do we know who owns the land?'

'Consulting the Land Registry is on the list of jobs to do, sir, but the land isn't cultivated and contains a derelict house, which may or may not be connected with the case.' Hennessey then told Sharkey about the length of chain and the notches in the skirting board. He added that it would be his guess that the land was the subject of a long-running legal feud that was still unresolved and that would explain why it had not been developed or cultivated, and why the derelict building was not renovated while there was still time to save it. 'Now all you can do is demolish it.'

'If you get wind of an imminent demolition, you'd better halt it,' Sharkey said. 'Could be a crime scene, even if it's a crime scene of some twenty years previous, we don't want those fearsome yellow machines destroying what evidence there might still be in existence. That length of skirting board, for example, should we remove it?'

'Possibly, sir. But it's been photographed.'

'That wouldn't show that the links of the chain had caused the notches though, should it become an issue in any trial.'

'Good point, sir. I'll attend to it.'

'But yes, I think you ought to sweep the area while there's daylight left to do so. I'll leave it up to you to liaise with the uniformed branch.'

One hour later, George Hennessey, one sergeant and twenty constables were back on the waste ground. Within one hour of arriving, they had located three more house bricks, each covered with fading white paint or whitewash. Each location was marked with a pole three feet in length which was driven firmly into the ground close by each brick. The area was then designated a crime scene and one constable, equipped with radio, was left to guard the area until the end of his shift when, at 10 p.m., he would be relieved by another constable to stand the night watch from 10 until 6 a.m.

Hennessey returned to Micklegate Bar Police Station and saw Yellich had added recording in the file on the as yet unidentified murder victim, detailing the post-mortem findings: young, white, female, slain with a massive blow to the skull. Age yet to be determined, report will be faxed a.s.a.p. He took the file and placed it in his filing cabinet and locked it. He signed out in order to return home. He stepped into the car park at the rear of the building and, anticipating the rush hour of cars presently nose to tailing their way out of the ancient city, he chose, on a whim, to visit YO26.

He walked down Blossom Street, crossed the road, took the right turn into Holgate Road and walked along it until the ribbon of tarmac became Poppleton Road. He was then in Holgate proper as darkness fell along with a soft, gentle, but relentless rainfall that caused the street lamps to assume haloes around them, and caused the pavements and the road surface to glisten. The houses were uniformly terraced houses which abutted on to the pavement without even the most modest of front gardens. It was an area of blind corners, of shadows, of dark places, of muted lights from within the houses, from the occasional pub and the late-opening corner shops. Folk were in the street and from it he could read the nature of the community: working men carrying canvas knapsacks, mixed with

41

overweight women in plastic headscarves riding bicycles, who mixed with youths, casually dressed, speaking in plummy boarding-school southern-county accents. These last, Hennessey knew, were students of the ilk of the four who had been reported missing, about twenty years ago in the case of the latest to vanish without trace, and nearly thirty years ago in the case of the first to be reported missing. All four, Hennessey thought, would be like these young ones, loving the student life, away from home, no pressure except that of their studies, possibly angst-ridden because of forming and breaking of human relationships, enthusiastic about their futures and then they had, it appears, been abducted. What was it that Michael Henderson had given on their description? Two well-built men, one very small man and a woman, also small. Sufficient to overpower a woman on a dark street? But she would scream, the alarm would have been raised, so how else could a young woman be abducted . . . ensnared by some means, perhaps, but such young women are always, in his experience, very well warned and would be suspicious of any lure . . . the woman of the group? Could she have been the bait? A woman would go to the assistance of any other woman who appeared to be in distress . . . but one step at a time, and twenty to thirty years after the crimes in question, the chances of finding the culprits was remote.

Very remote, indeed.

Hennessey, his collar turned up against the rain, and sparing a passing thought for the constable who at that moment was mounting his lonely vigil on the waste ground by the derelict house, returned to Micklegate Bar Police Station, to his car in the car park and drove home, the rush hour by then having eased sufficiently to allow him to drive in heavy but free-flowing traffic.

He drove out to Easingwold, and to his detached four-bedroomed house on the Thirsk Road and parked his car in the driveway. At his arrival, Oscar, his brown mongrel, barked excitedly and turned joyfully in the back garden, prevented from running and jumping up at Hennessey by a wire fence. Hennessey let himself into his house by the front door, where he was fully greeted by Oscar, who had entered the house via the dog flap and intercepted him in the hallway. He patted his dog and toyed with his ears. He picked up his mail, then walked into the kitchen and, as if on automatic pilot, he switched on the electric kettle and, walking past it, opened the backdoor of the house and looked out across the lawn, with a gate set in the middle to allow access to the orchard beyond the lawn and to the 'going forth' beyond the orchard. Feeling disinclined to walk out into the rain, he stood at the rear door and said, 'Hello, Jen, some day today, it really was. Early in the piece still, but what a piece it turned out to be. More digging tomorrow . . . after all, if they're under the house bricks they've been down there for nearly thirty years, well in one case anyway. I don't think one more day is going to make a deal of difference, and we would have had to do it by arc light as well, had we started today. This rain will prove useful too, soften up the ground, make it easier for the boys. Take care.'

He closed the door and made himself a simple but wholesome meal of grilled pork chops and vegetables. No dessert, just the main meal, survival cooking like any, at least many, he thought, single men. He spent the evening re-reading an ordinary soldier's account of the Battle of Gettysburg. Such simple language, and such attention to detail, that the piece thrilled him. Later he fed and exercised Oscar, the rain by then having eased slightly but it didn't take much for Hennessey to coax

Oscar outside. His dog, like all dogs, loved his evening walk, but this dog, like all dogs, was miserable in the rain, and when the rain was torrential, he would not allow himself to be dragged from the house. But that evening his resistance was only nominal, and man and dog walked out for half an hour, then back for half an hour. Later still he strolled into Easingwold, to the Dove Inn, for a pint of Brown and Mild, just one, before last orders were called.

'Anamnesis.' The woman folded her legs under her and curled up with her husband on the settee. The lights were dim, Bach played softly, outside a dog barked, and further away a car drove away, a little too fast for the streets and with sloppy change from first to second gear. The man cocked a professional ear at the sound of the car: a drunk driver, but it was not his concern that night. 'Knew there was a word for it, remembered from the dim and distant. Psychologists call it "recovered memory", but the ancient Greeks knew all about it and had a word for it.'

'Anamnesis,' the man echoed and held his wife in a strong, but gentle, arm.

'Well, that's the English translation. It means something from the past come to live in the present.'

Somerled Yellich had returned from the York District Hospital, placed the pen with productions, added Dr D'Acre's findings to the recording in the still thin file on the human remains found that morning. He had placed the file on DCI Hennessey's desk, signed out and had returned home, most grateful to do so. It was, after all, his favourite journey by far. He drove out of York with the rush-hour traffic to the village of Huntingdon, on the more sought-after northern side of the city, and at Huntingdon had turned into a small, neat-looking side road, which led into a new build estate, and to his home, his wife and his son. Jeremy had run to meet him and had collided with his father with such force that Yellich was nearly knocked off his feet, but Jeremy was twelve years old now, and a large, heavy twelve at that. He had inherited his father's size. Inside the house, Sara had thrown a weary, powdery arm round her husband's shoulder and had kissed him.

'Bad day?' he asked, sensing the fatigue.

'He's been impossible . . . I'm sure he's a lunatic, meant correctly, of course.'

'Of course.' Yellich knew his wife and mother of their first and only begotten better than to even think that she would be disparaging towards him. 'But it isn't even close to a full moon.'

'Well, he has moods that I can't predict. Came back from school as though he had been given a fix of adrenalin, took hours to calm him, even had to give in and let him have the television. He won.' She shrugged her shoulders. 'I know what we agreed, I know what the clinic says, television is to be earned by good behaviour, not used to buy off bad behaviour. The theory is fine, but they don't have to put it into practice. He was running around, wouldn't settle . . . so I turned it on and he settled instantly, even though I doubt he can make out what's on the screen, not fully anyway . . .' Then she sobbed and Yellich held her while she wept, until his shirt was saturated.

Yellich had then gone into the lounge and switched off the television, and had sat Jeremy at the table and kept him there until he could point to every letter of the alphabet when it was dictated randomly, and until he could tell the time correctly when asked to do so by the clock kept for educational purposes. Then he was allowed a little more television before supper and bed. With love, 'supportive discipline' and stimulation, the Yellichs had been told that by the time their son was twenty, he should have achieved the mental age of twelve and be able to live a semi-independent existence in a hostel, his own room, self-catering, if he wished, but staff on hand at all times.

Later that night Somerled and Sara Yellich had curled up together on the sofa, sipping wine, as music played softly.

'I would have been a head of department by now if I hadn't allowed you to drag me by the hair into this bottomless pit yclept marriage.'

'Not much dragging involved, as I recall,' Yellich had said, 'and about as much hair to drag with as today. Have I told you—'

'When you first saw me, you thought I was a fella . . . yes, often, thank you. So, I'm not curvy . . .'

'Suits me . . . successful men are attracted to women with slender figures.'

'In-service training tell you that?'

'Magazine at the dentist's, actually.' Then he had told her about his day, about the drunkard who had remembered something after twenty years, and what had happened as a consequence.

'Ah . . .' Sara Yellich raised her head slightly, 'I know a word for that . . . ancient Greek word. Oh, what is it? It'll come . . . meaning coming from the past to live in the present . . . that's annoyed me now. What is it? It'll come . . . So you attended the PM; what then?'

Three

*In which Yellich visits a Pear in Knaresborough,
more skeletons are unearthed, and Hennessey
once again hears of his senior officer's 'ghosts'.*

'Never thought I'd see one of those again.' The man
held the small ballpoint which was encased in a
clear cellophane sachet.

'You did distribute them?'

'Twenty years ago. Are you sure it's one of ours? The
writing isn't clear.'

'Yes, our people at Wetherby were able to enhance the
writing.'

'It was gold on black. Yes, you can still just make it
out.' The man was elderly, short, portly, thick-framed
lenses, but gratifyingly, to Yellich, still possessed his
faculties. He had also evidently done well in life and
was now living in clearly very comfortable retirement
in a large, expansive but, to Yellich's taste, rather squat
bungalow near the racecourse. 'How can I help you?' He
handed the pen back to Yellich.

'By telling us all you can about the pen.'

'Well, come in.' The man stepped aside and allowed
Yellich to enter his home. Yellich found it neat, well
ordered, smelling of polish and air freshener. 'This way,
please.' The man ambled down what seemed to Yellich

47

to be a corridor too narrow for the size of the house, and turned into a room that revealed itself to be the lounge, with a vast window that looked out on to a lawn, on which a late-middle-aged lady was playing ball with two young children. The man sat and, noticing Yellich's gaze turning towards the garden, he said, 'The grandchildren. Too young to attend school yet, so we look after them during the day, while their parents are at work. Take a seat please.'

Yellich sat on a leather settee, which squeaked as he did so. The room had a wall-to-wall carpet in brown, giving to a pastel-shaded wallpaper of a lilac colour. China vases and other ornaments decorated the room, a Brueghel print hung above the mantelpiece. Beside the fireplace was a modern television set, hugely expensive, much, much wider than it was deep. On the other side of the fireplace stood an equally expensive looking hi-fi system. A coffee table stood in the middle of the room, on which were copies of *Country Life* and *Country Walking*. The couple were clearly still enjoying some youth.

'How did you find me anyway?'

'We phoned the company Soundings Ltd, as it said on the pen. The phone number on the pen is no longer used, so we tried Directory Enquiries and they gave us the new number of the company . . . phoned them, they gave us your number and address, explaining that the pen was about twenty years old.'

'They shouldn't have done that. I'll phone their MD when I can. I have a right to have my privacy respected.'

'You do indeed, sir, but we did impress upon them that it was a police inquiry into a very serious crime.'

'Serious?'

'Murder.'

'Ah . . .' The man sat back in his chair and put his

finger across his mouth in a pensive gesture. 'Doesn't get more serious.'

'Not much, anyway.' Yellich adjusted his position and again caused the leather to squeak.

'Don't get self-conscious about the sound – visitors do but my wife and I no longer notice it.'

Yellich smiled, gratified by the release of tension. 'So you are the owner of Soundings Ltd?'

'I was. It's a geological survey company, send soundwaves into the ground, reveals rock strata . . . travelled all over the world . . . usually searching for black gold.'

'Black gold?'

'Oil. Sometimes we searched for gas. Often looked for one, found the other, or found them both in the same place, as in the North Sea, though Sounding didn't find those deposits. I mention the North Sea as an example of oil and gas being found together.'

'I see.'

'Soundings can only search on terra firma. Other companies have equipment to scan below the seabed, but not Soundings. But to answer your question, I was the owner and Managing Director of Soundings. I started the company with second-hand equipment and some borrowed capital when I was still in my twenties. It brought me a good income and, like I said, I have travelled globally because of it. Sold up when I turned sixty, the whole kit and caboodle, turned everything over to a rival outfit, kept a large amount of shares, but the selling price . . . well, I did very well. Can't complain. The rivals kept the company as it was, and run it as an independent concern.'

'Competing with their own business?'

'In a sense, but not exclusively, there are many such

companies and the market is literally global. Penn and Swannell, the rival company, operate Soundings as an independent concern, expecting it to show a profit, but keep Soundings' operations away from Penn and Swannell's. Soundings, for example, is opening up markets in Eastern Europe and the Russian Federation, not properly surveyed, even now, and Penn and Swannell are letting them get on with it. But any profit will eventually find its way into Penn and Swannell's coffers.'

'I see. So, the pen?'

'The pen – well, I know nothing of that individual pen, but the batch it was part of was a promotional idea. We were approached by a company that buys pens like that in bulk from the manufacturers and embosses the names of other companies on them to sell them to those other companies as promotional gimmicks. We bought a batch of two hundred.'

'Was that considered large?'

'Too large really. We had a small workforce, customers tend to be large oil companies and foreign governments, and giving silly little ballpoints to executives and dignitaries and ministers is quite offensive. People like that are used to bigger and better freebies to oil the wheels of business. Two days shoot on a grouse moor is more the sort of freebie they're used to. Giving them pens like that is likely to be counterproductive. It was, you may see, a very ill-advised purchase. And because of that we tended to give them out to more lowly folk.'

'More lowly?'

'Lowly like me, my wife, our friends, relatives, the workforce, emphasizing that it was for their children, not for them, so as to make the gift acceptable without being patronizing or demeaning. The gardeners got some, as did the cleaning staff.'

'The gardeners here, or at the company premises?'

'Both. The company premises had, still have, a small garden to the front, a lawn and a flowerbed that have to be maintained. We have a vast garden – what you see is only about a third of our land. We have badgers in our garden. From our land they can get on to the racecourse and forage there but their sets are in our land, patrolled by two Dobermanns at night, so nobody will bait our badgers. The Dobermanns leave them alone, sensibly – badger on Dobermann, the Dobermann will take the second prize. But the Dobermanns keep the humans out. The house and the company are cleaned by contractors, and we gave the cleaners the pens. Promotional gimmicks like that are intended to get the company's name known where it needs to be known. All that purchase did was to get the name known in schools and ordinary households in and around York.'

'I see . . .' Yellich was disappointed.

'Drawing a blank, fella?'

''Fraid I am, sir.'

'Is the pen the only lead you've got?'

'Pretty well.' Again he shifted his position, again the leather sofa squeaked, but mindful of Mr Forester's earlier advice, Yellich did not feel embarrassed by causing the sound. 'The victim was a young woman, murdered about twenty years ago, buried in a shallow grave . . . out between here and Selby and this was found in her mouth.' He tapped the pen. 'It's been examined, taken apart, nothing inside the plastic casing.'

'In her mouth?'

'Yes.' Yellich held eye contact with Forester, who had paled at the news. 'She clearly knew she was going to be killed and she found a way of leaving us a present. The person, or persons, who murdered her had some

51

connection with Soundings Ltd. She was able to pick up this pen and keep it concealed, we don't know how long for, and pop it into her mouth shortly before she was murdered.'

'Speaks for a high level of intelligence, and foresight . . . generous-spirited.'

'Well, if she is who we think she is, she was one of four students who disappeared over a nearly nine-year period, about twenty years ago.'

'Don't remember that being reported.'

'It wasn't, the disappearances were not linked at the time, possibly are not linked; we are groping in the dark.'

'Well, let me help you all I can.' Forester ran his fingers through his hair, balding in places, untidily long in others. 'We only made one purchase of those pens, for reasons explained and also because they proved to be of poor quality, lasting only a week or two before drying up. I doubt if the paperwork in respect of the purchase is still available, in fact it won't be. But if by some means I can remember when we received delivery of them, that young woman would have been murdered when those pens were still in use, which would be within two weeks of them being distributed . . . and we gave them to the twenty employees of the company, the gardeners here and at the company, the domestics, here and at the company, and to personal friends. That is not an inexhaustible number of people.'

Yellich smiled at him. 'You would have made a good detective, sir.'

'Well . . . I am reluctant to provide you with the names of personal friends, in fact I won't, unless you slap me with a warrant.'

'Understood.'

'But my friends wouldn't do anything like that anyway.'

Yellich remained silent but pondered how wealthy he'd be if he could have a twenty pound note for every time he'd heard that sentiment expressed. The person only to be later shown that friends or relatives were indeed very, very capable of doing something like that.

'So . . . you know I can pin down the date of the receipt of the pens. I remember giving my nephew one . . . one of my sisters married a New Zealander, an insurance broker in Auckland, they visited about that time, my nephew was then about nine or ten. He's a married man now, one child so far . . . when did they visit? It was when I was negotiating for a contract in the Gulf.' Forester stood. 'Just a moment please, I'll have to get my journals.'

Alone in the room Yellich relaxed back on the settee and looked around the room. It was wide, generously proportioned in terms of floor area, but the ceiling he found to be oppressively low, so low that he, a tall man, fancied he could reach it with fingertips if on tip-toe. Outside, the woman still played ball and seemed to show no interest in him, a stranger in her house, if indeed she could see him because it then occurred to Yellich that while he could see out, by some phenomenon of angle of sun on glass, she might not be able to see in. He remained seated, patiently, happy to do so because Mr Forester was proving to be wholly co-operative. Forester returned a few moments later holding a bundle of diaries.

'Daily journals.' He held them up, smiling. 'Had a strange experience once.' He sat in the chair, lightly so, thought Yellich, for such a heavy-looking man of rotundity. 'I was clearing my father's house. We all have that sad experience, those of us who do the right thing and don't predecease our parents – a very poignant experience . . . have you?'

'Yes,' Yellich said. 'Both my parents are now deceased. I cleared their house . . . it is a life experience, as you say.'

'And you came across things from your own child-hood?'

'Oh yes . . . things I'd forgotten.'

'As I did. I found a diary given as a stocking filler when I was about fifteen and I made entries on a daily basis up to about the twentieth of January, and I read it . . . three weeks of my life some twenty years earlier . . . it was eerie, so absorbing. Anyway, I found that old diary of mine in the December of that year and so on the first of January next, I began a daily journal and have not missed a single day, not one single day in nearly thirty years. My wife says it's in case I need an alibi, in case I get arrested.'

Yellich smiled.

'But really it's a need to record, almost compulsive . . . and I am so pleased I did, because occasionally I take a year at random and recollect what I did one week. It's more immediate than looking at old photographs.'

'I can believe that.' Yellich thought the word 'immediacy' perfect for describing the feeling he often experienced when reading old police files.

'Let me see . . .' Forester sat with a diary open in front of him, others, about six, in a pile on the floor. He leafed through the diary and put it on the floor mumbling 'not that year', picked up the next diary from the pile, and did the same. It was the fourth diary that contained the information sought. Forester beamed at Yellich. 'July, twenty years ago. I know it was a summer – it made sense to visit in the English summer and my nephew was having an extended holiday. He remarked that it was like having two summers . . . so the girl was murdered about that time.'

'July, twenty years ago.'

'Well, I gave my nephew's son a couple of the pens as a keepsake. We'd just received delivery and I was handing them out left, right and centre, but not to clients.'

'As you said, the workforce, contracted cleaners, contract gardeners.'

'And the family, as in the case of my nephew from NZ.'

'Did you have a large workforce?'

'What is large?'

'How many employees?'

'Thanks. I prefer easily understood questions. Not many, about twenty, as I said.'

'Not many at all.'

'Well, admin and clerical, who never left the office to do work, numbered about five . . . and technicians to operate the equipment in the field and "gaffers" to lift it.'

'Gaffers?'

'We borrowed the term from the film industry, if you have ever wondered what a "gaffer" is as the credits roll, it's a very strong man who lifts the equipment that is very heavy. "Gaffers" are also minders to the equipment and guard it jealously. The "key grip" can only operate the camera once the "gaffer" has set it up and the "best boy" is a sort of eager gaffer who is making a start in the business and runs errands and does odd jobs. "Gaffers" and "key grips" all start as "best boy". So we had the technicians, the "gaffers" and we even had a "best boy" and me, so about fifteen formed the field survey team. The pens I gave to the gardeners and domestics, and I remember the names of the domestics but the gardeners, two blokes, I just handed them a handful of pens and said, "Here you are, something for your children," hoping a little bit of extra effort would go into the garden that day.'

'Which gardening service was that, do you recall?'

'Ace of Spades.'

'Ingenious name.' Yellich wrote the name down in his pad.

'It is rather. My favourite is a ladies' hairdressers called Curl Up and Dye.'

'I once knew a fish and chip shop called Jaws,' Yellich offered. 'But I must see if the Ace of Spades company is still operating.'

'Confess I haven't seen them advertising, which is strange because gardening is a nice line to be in. What with our ageing population, all those suburban gardens to be maintained. Good, healthy outdoor activity. I can think of worse things to do if you are self-employed. It'll be cigars in the summer and roll-ups in the winter but you'd survive . . . provenly so, by the number of people advertising gardening services in the local free sheet.'

'And the names of the employees at the time?'

'They'll be in the company archives.'

'OK, no problem there.'

'Ought not to be, given the ease with which they gave you my address. That annoys me. Did you ask for me personally?'

'Not in so many words, sir. Just said we were making enquiries about a pen bearing the company name that is connected with a crime of about twenty years ago, and the person to whom we spoke said we would be better talking to you. She seemed to know about the pens.'

'She . . . that'll be Agnes. My, is she still employed? She'll be nearing retiring age now . . . a telephonist and a very good one. She just had one of those magpie minds, pick anything up and store it away, and remembering a batch of pens that arrived twenty years ago . . . that's just Agnes, and helpful too . . . yes, I can see Agnes just wanting to please and being a little too free with information. So it was Agnes you spoke to. I'm not so annoyed now.'

'I hope not, sir. I wouldn't want to be the cause of any ill feeling.'

'Hardly your fault if you are, but I wouldn't worry.'

'The domestics now. Do you recall their names?'

'Mrs Brown did for us at the time. She is no longer with us. And I have to confess that I doubt she would have been a profitable line of inquiry anyway. She had only very distant relatives, lived alone, always keen to get here and reluctant to leave, always finding extra jobs to do to extend her working day. I gave her about half a dozen pens but she seemed puzzled as to what to do with them and only years later it occurred to me that she was illiterate and had been hiding the fact. The pens became a source of concern and worry for her, as though by their presence, the illiteracy might be exposed.'

'I see.' Yellich, having written Mrs Brown on his pad, crossed her name out. 'That leaves the cleaners at the workplace.'

'Steps and Stairs,' Forester replied quickly. 'Still in operation. Don't know if they keep archives. Cleaners don't stay often, a few months as a rule.'

'We can only check and see.'

'I can't recall their Christian names. Molly was there at the time because she had a son who had emigrated to New Zealand. I remember having a chat with her . . . but as for the others, sorry, can't help you there.'

'You have been more than helpful as it is.' Yellich

closed his notepad, and stood. 'Thank you. It is appreci-
ated. Your wife doesn't seem curious about me?'

'Melanie . . . she can't see you. She's blind. Car
accident when in her twenties, the ball they're playing
with, it has a bell inside it.'

It was a pleasant day. Hennessey thought it so. The
relentless wind of the previous day, which had moaned
across the Vale under a low sky, had on Tuesday given
way to what was widely recognized to be the last of the
summer weather, a high sky of white cloud, about five
tenths in airforce speak, a hot sun that exploited the gaps
in the cloud to bake the land below, and no wind, no wind
at all. The foliage, though, betrayed the time of year and
was, upon the trees, a gentle mix of green and brown,
mostly brown. Occasionally a small darting movement
of grey caught Hennessey's eye: a squirrel, feverishly
busy. It spoke of a hard winter to come. It would, in
other circumstances, be a pleasant day to be away from
his desk for an hour or two, but the circumstances were,
in fact, hardly pleasant. He stood on the waste ground,
between Mallard's Car Depot and the derelict house, where
the previous day the skeleton of a young female had been
unearthed. He had arrived at the scene earlier that morning
with twenty constables and a sergeant, and three large
blue and white inflatable tents and six wheelbarrows.
The tents had been inflated, one each over where the
white painted house bricks had been found and covered
an area of about four hundred square feet. Constables dug
with spades, not clumsily as the constables had done the
previous day, but carefully, somewhat ironically thought
Hennessey, or maybe perhaps appropriately, like a grave-
digger would toil at his craft, keeping the sides vertical
and the base of the hole horizontal, slicing away the soil

layer, rather than driving vertically like a navvy. Each layer of soil was levered into a wheelbarrow where it was sifted for any item, any artefact that might be deemed to be significant, each barrow full of soil was then wheeled out of the inflatable tent to an area, designated by the sergeant, where it was tipped, and other constables subjected the soil to a second, detailed fingertip search. It took two hours of careful painstaking digging by four constables before the first skeleton was exposed. It was exposed as the skeleton found the previous day had been exposed, a round, whitened object that didn't give to the spade and that might have been a stone, and that, like the hard, rounded, whitened object discovered yesterday, revealed itself to be a skull.

The find was reported to DI Hennessey, who walked to the tent together with the Scenes of Crime Officer and in the tent, hat removed, he stood and observed the careful inch by inch exposure of the second skeleton to be found buried in that particular area of land. Periodically the constables would step out of the hole they had carefully excavated to allow the Scenes of Crime Officer to photograph the skeleton, so that its exposure, inch by inch, was captured, frame by frame in both colour and black and white photographs to form evidence that would, Hennessey hoped, one day form part of a 'bundle' to be laid before each juror at a hearing of the High Court presided over by a judge cloaked in scarlet with cuffs of ermine. Wherein a black-gowned, bewigged QC would, with a calm voice of educated tones, say, 'If I could ask the jurors to turn to pages ten to twenty of their bundle, they will see photographs showing the exposure of a skeleton, which we will show proved to be the body of X.' It is by such meticulous, careful recording of the crime scene, and exposure of evidence, that cases are won when it comes to the trial of the accused. The case for the Crown is built as evidence is discovered, detail by detail. The skeleton was carefully exposed and when fully exposed, it was seen lying on its front, head twisted to one side, teeth grinning, it seemed, and hands fastened together in the front by a short piece of lightweight chain and two small padlocks.

'Leave her like that,' Hennessey said. 'Her, because it will be a female. The forensic pathologist will want to start work with the skeleton as it is, and she'll have to supervise the lifting. Right, vacate the tent please, one constable to remain at the door to prevent unauthorized entry. Thanks all, that was a good job done. Excellent job, in fact.'

Hennessey walked to his car, radioed Micklegate Bar Police Station and asked for his compliments to be conveyed to Dr Louise D'Acre at the Department of Pathology, York City Hospital, her attendance is required . . . the same location as yesterday. Hennessey added, 'Dr D'Acre will know where to find us.'

One hour later, Dr D'Acre parked her car behind the police vehicles and walked, black bag in hand, to where Hennessey stood.

'Three tents?' she observed.

'One for each skeleton, Dr D'Acre,' Hennessey replied solemnly. 'Since I called, asking for you to attend, two more skeletons have been found. The field is giving up its dead.'

'A field of dark secrets.' Louise D'Acre grimaced and raised her right eyebrow. Hennessey nodded grimly, and their brief, split-second eye contact was instantly broken by Louise D'Acre. 'Well, any one you'd like me to look at before the other two?'

'No, nothing to say from the police point of view that

any one warrants your attention before any other. All skeletons, all about the same distance down, all with wrists bound with chains, in front of them.'

'And all female,' D'Acre said as she stepped out of the third tent, 'all young adult, all with massive head injuries, consistent with being hit from behind with the blade of a shovel, as your witness of yesterday indicated had been the method of dispatch of the first victim to be found. Nothing back from the lab yet re poison or age of death.'

'I see.'

'Expecting that at any time, might be in my in box now.'

'Good, that'll help us identify the young women. Age at death, we can link to age at disappearance from the mis per files, hopefully get dental records . . .'

'Yes . . . did you get any metal near the bones?'

'Metal?' Hennessey shielded his eyes from a sudden glare as the sun was exposed by cloud movement.

'Zip fasteners, bra hooks?'

'Don't think so . . . we haven't searched the soil beneath the bones yet though, anything like that might have sunk there through time.'

'If you don't it means they were naked when they were murdered and buried, certainly when they were buried. Textiles from clothing would have disappeared if they were all buried about the same time as the skeleton of the person we found yesterday had been murdered, but metal would survive.'

'We didn't . . . no jewellery, come to think of it, no watches, bracelets, earrings, everything must have been taken from them.'

Louise D'Acre shuddered. She had learned to become dispassionate when determining the cause of death, to muster clinical detachment, even to allow humour into her work, being particularly fond of saying that her patients are the only sort who don't feel pain and are guaranteed not to register a complaint about her with the British Medical Association, but insights into her patients' last hours, or days, would still reach her, as with four young women who had been stripped of everything, even their jewellery, and kept chained in a derelict house for days before being murdered. And it especially reached her that one of the young women, at least one, had given up hope of being rescued or of escaping, but had managed to conceal the casing of a small ballpoint pen in her mouth, something to guide the police to her murderer, or murderers. She asked about the pen.

'Yellich's chasing it up at the moment,' Hennessey replied. 'I'll see him at lunch. I'll let you know what, if anything, he has found.'

'I'd be interested.' Dr D'Acre adjusted her footing on an uneven surface of the field. 'This case emerges above the rest at the moment.'

'Busy?'

'Road traffic accident . . .' Her voice trailed off. 'Sorry . . .'

Hennessey smiled. 'That's OK. Been a long time, but people's passion for cars, especially young people's passion for fast cars, is something I'll never fathom.'

'Fathom?' D'Acre smiled. 'You've been in Yorkshire too long. Nobody would believe you're a Londoner. Anyway, if you've finished here, I'll have the skeletons removed to York City. Will you be attending for the police?'

'Yes, I will. Sergeant Yellich did it yesterday, he'll still have the sweet smell of formaldehyde in his nostrils. My turn now. Besides, I want him to check the Land

Registry. I want to know who owns yon.' He nodded at the derelict house.

'Yes.' Louise D'Acre followed his gaze. 'That house has a history . . . and I don't just mean its age. Probably a recent history, but there is an atmosphere about that house, I picked it up yesterday.'

'Probably nothing to do with the owners, but we'll check anyway.'

'OK. So, if I start the post-mortems at two p.m., would that suit the police?'

'That would suit the police admirably.' Hennessey smiled at the slender, short-haired doctor of forensic pathology and this time, upon their parting, his eye contact was allowed. Briefly.

Yellich visited the Land Registry in the municipal Library of York. A waif-like, almost anorexic, he thought, bespectacled woman warmly asked if she could be of assistance. He produced a map of the area of police interest on which he had marked the boundary of the area of waste ground, and the derelict house. The woman asked Yellich if she could 'keep hold' of the map for a minute or two. Yellich nodded, said 'happily' and she turned and walked away from the reception desk. Yellich wandered away from the desk, looking at posters, and notices, and promotional literature. Moments later the woman returned to the reception desk and handed the map back to Yellich. She also handed him a computer printout. 'We would have had to spend hours leafing through ledgers in the old days,' she said, 'but here you are. Five acres of pasture plus house, bordering Sheepcote Lane, off the A24, Mallard's Auto Company and the farmland comprising part of Stubbs farm in the parish of Wilmington cum Lacy in the County of York.'

'Recognize Mallard's,' Yellich said. 'So it sounds right.'
'The deeds –' the woman pointed to a section of the
printout – 'are held by a firm of solicitors.'
'Pear and Co, Knaresborough,' Yellich read.
'That will mean the land is being conveyed or that the
ownership is in dispute.' The woman smiled. 'It means
that, one or the other.'
'Be the latter.' Yellich folded the computer printout and
put it in his pocket. 'The house is derelict and the land is
fallow, waste ground, hasn't seen a plough in years, or
a grazing herd either. But thanks, you have been very
helpful.'

Pear and Co of Knaresborough was a one-man operation that, by the appearance of Mr Pear, notary public,
well lived up to his name. He was a jocular man with a
heavily jowled face which seemed to widen from crown to
cheek and jaw, pear shaped, in fact, pondered Yellich. The
torso too was of a pear shape, a bald head atop a massive,
expansive body. But a silk shirt, and a very expensive
looking suit, a mahogany desk, oil paintings on the wall,
which to Yellich's untrained eye looked original and were
probably very valuable, spoke of a man of considerable
wealth, the very embodiment of the oft heard observation
that 'you never meet a poor solicitor'.

'Quite a dispute.' Benjamin Pear, for that was the name
upon the nameplate upon his desk, had a soft voice,
'very plummy', thought Yellich, very public-school and
illustrious university voice. 'Been dragging on for years,
complicated because the two parties live on opposite sides
of the planet. The story in a nutshell is that the family grew
up in the old house that is on the land in question . . . have
you visited it?'

Yellich said he had.

'I understand it's derelict?'

'Very . . . you can still make out the shape of a house but that's about all.'

'I see . . . that accords with the reports I've received. No need for me to visit it, you see.'

'Of course, sir.' Yellich glanced out of the window behind Pear, cluttered red rooftops of Knaresborough, looking out towards Harrogate, blue sky, clouds moving a little faster than they had moved that morning.

'The family, with the inappropriate name of Smiley, lived there as the old house fell down around them. A very eccentric family, very oddball, lived off a legacy left by a relative of an earlier era. Apparently always seen together, had an old car and would drive to Selby to buy in their weekly provisions and they would be seen no more until their next weekly visit. No television in the home, no hot running water, no nothing. Anyway, the old boy passed away and the two sons refused to attend the funeral. Just a coffin and a priest at the funeral . . . and then the two sons, by then in their late thirties, started fighting. It was as if the old boy had kept the lid on a powder keg and when he was no longer, said keg exploded. The issue was that he died intestate, always complicates things. I hope you have made a will, young fella?'

'I have.'

'Good, good . . . makes things a lot easier, less work for the likes of me and my kind, but easier for all others. Anyway, the fight was about the fact that both of the brothers claim that their father had said he was to have the property in its entirety and the other brother was to be cast out into the wilderness without a penny to his name.'

'Each brother contended that the land is his in its entirety?'

'Yes, exactly. Neither can corroborate his claims. The sensible thing to do would be to sell the land and house, derelict, and divide the proceeds, but we are not dealing with a sensible family. They are eccentric to the point of being certifiably insane. So the two brothers, by now in their sixties, are both living in poverty, one in Canada, and the other in Australia, and are content to live in poverty rather than each relinquish his claim to the land in question, in full. So the land and the property upon said land is as you find it today.'

'I see.' Yellich pondered the pigheadedness of the brothers. Very Yorkshire, he thought. It was his observation that generalizations can be made about the peoples of this isle – that music seems to reach more deeply into the soul of a Welshman than any other, that a Scot has a fiery temper, and that Yorkshire people invented pigheadedness, and this was pigheadedness in the extreme, doubtless exacerbated by the other trait of people of this county, being their ability to bear a grudge and do so for periods measured in years. So these two brothers were probably living as described because they had fallen out over the use of a toy when they were children. 'So, the real question of interest for the police, Mr Pear, is when did the property become vacant . . . i.e. when was it abandoned?'

'When the brothers physically removed themselves, you mean?'

'Yes.'

'Different concept from abandoning.' Pear smiled. 'In the eyes of the law it is not an abandoned property, but the two brothers turned the key for the last time the day after their father's funeral.' Pear leaned forward and consulted the thick file that lay on his desk. 'Oh my, thirty-one years ago today. Have I been in practice that long? The Smileys were one of my first clients. Thirty-one years in the practice, behind this desk . . .

took over from my father when he retired. Oh my . . . thirty-one years.'

'Big case?' Commander Sharkey leaned back in his chair.

'Bigger than we thought, sir.' George Hennessey also relaxed but clasped his hands together, as he always found he did when in the presence of authority. Even when the figure of authority was, as in this instance, much younger than he.

'Four skeletons?'

'Four, all female.'

'Any more in there, do you think?'

'Well, sir . . .' Hennessey looked down and again pondered the liver spots on the back of his hands. 'Frankly only ground radar will tell us that, and the approval for the cost will have to come from you, and I know how tight the budget is.'

'It's remained the same cash amount for three years despite escalating costs. Off the record, I got told I'm here to manage, so manage. That's what they say, on the phone of course. Official memos are just official gobbledegook but essentially the message is just the same. So unless there is any indication of more bad news in the shape of human remains buried in the field you tell me about, I don't think I'll be wearing the cost of ground radar.'

'Frankly, I don't think there is, sir.' Hennessey held eye contact with the more youthful, much smaller and impeccably turned out Sharkey. His desk too, Hennessey always thought, was neat, even for a police officer, and he shuddered to think what kind of house Sharkey ran. He had never met Sharkey's wife, nor his children, for Sharkey kept home and his office very, very separate. He rarely attended social functions, like retirement parties, and if he did, he put in a brief appearance for form's sake, had one non-alcoholic drink, took his very proper leave of the person in whose honour the party was being thrown, and left. Hennessey imagined a repressive husband with a whimpering wife and frightened children. Yet what made the man human was that he was haunted; his sense of ethics had been compromised. It was for that reason that Hennessey suspected he had been asked to 'pop' into Sharkey's office. As most often in such instances, it was Hennessey's experience that the good commander would spend some time enquiring about prominent, current investigations before striking at the heart of the matter. 'You see, sir –' Hennessey unclasped his hands – 'each body seemed to be marked, that is the grave seemed to be marked with an ordinary house brick, which had been painted with white paint or whitewash. Only four such house bricks were found.'

'I see.'

'Not even other house bricks that had not been painted were found. Someone wanted to mark the graves.'

'For what purpose?'

'For no other purpose than wanting to return to the scene of the crime would be my guess.'

'A murderer will always return to the scene of his crime, you mean?'

'Or her crime, but yes, that's what I mean. One of the earliest gems of criminal profiling but, yes, that's the only reason I can see. They appeared to have been buried randomly . . . we have mapped the scene, of course.'

'Of course.'

'The sites of the graves don't form an identifiable pattern, not a square for example, or a straight line, or a cross, just random. The first grave to be discovered seems to be a little more separate than the rest, a little more out on its own, the other three forming a loose cluster, seemingly so anyway, but really, I think it's a random scattering.'

'I see.'

'The other thing that makes me believe that there are no more shallow graves in the area is that four young women were reported disappearing over a nine-year period at about the time our informant recalls seeing one girl murdered.'

'Those disappearances were not connected?'

'No, sir. Embarrassing for us, but no. All the detectives who worked the cases are now retired and no work was done anyway, save taking details, as is procedure. But those details may now prove vital to identifying the bodies.'

'Indeed . . . indeed, but even so, four young women disappear in York, and nobody links the disappearances?'

'It must have been the time gap between the disappearances, sir, and the old, but valid, excuse of overstretched, overworked police officers, and different officers working each case . . . no overview . . . that only came in the fullness of time . . . now they can be linked. All four were students, all lived in the same area of the city.'

'But even so, it's a city in name only, it isn't a throbbing metropolis of a place.'

'Different faculties, different colleges even. One girl was a student at the Teacher Training College, another was a student at the Academy of Music and Drama . . . the two university students disappeared seven years apart and attended different faculties . . . the only people who should have seen a link was either ourselves or the press.'

'What is the link, apart from age, sex?'

'That they all lived in Holgate, YO26 . . . that they all disappeared in the winter of the year, all were last seen in the early evening . . . as if abducted off dark streets. And Holgate can be very dark indeed.'

'Any link at all with the owner of the land?'

'DS Yellich chased that up this morning, sir. I saw him just before lunch. He uncovered a grim story of an isolated and dysfunctional family who inhabited the house on the land, but who provenly abandoned the house upon the death of the father. The two brothers moving as far apart from each other as they could.'

'Far?'

'Canada and Australia.'

'That's far enough!' Sharkey allowed himself a brief and rare smile.

'The first girl of the four to be reported missing was reported two years after the house was abandoned, by which time the brothers were in different hemispheres, on different continents, communicating with each other via their solicitor in historic and picturesque Knaresborough. But Yellich did postulate something of interest.'

'Oh . . . ?'

'Yes . . . he pointed out that the house was so remote that you'd have to know it existed, or the murderers chanced upon it while scouting for a remote location.'

'Good point.'

'I think so too, sir.' Hennessey paused. 'The only other establishment in the vicinity is a garage . . . not a repair garage with activity about it all day, but a storage garage . . . for Mallard's, in fact.'

'Oh yes, hire cars and second-hand cars of prestige.'

'The one, the same.'

'Really. I have looked at their list of cars for sale and have wondered where they are kept because their premises in York are quite modest in terms of space. Very nice location, but modest just the same.'

'Well, there's your answer, sir. They're all kept in a garage between York and Selby, well back from the main road. So we'll be looking at the employees of Mallard's when the young women disappeared. But keeping an open mind because the murderers may have chanced upon the site. We also have a pen, a small pen clearly a promotional device, which is linked to the murder.'

'Yes, I read that, very strong link, found in her mouth, leaving us a clue . . . brave girl. That's a stronger link than Mallard's.'

'Oh, much stronger, sir.'

'Good, please keep me informed . . . now, George.'

One hour later George Hennessey, having, he believed, placated and eased the troubled mind of his superior, and having diplomatically extracted himself from his presence, signed out and walked to York City Hospital. He crossed Micklegate Bar as the traffic lights halted the traffic and climbed up the steps on to the wall, as was his custom. He turned left on the wall and walked towards Lendal Bridge with the battlements to his left and a drop of some ten feet to a grass bank to his right. He pondered the fact that in summer the walls are thronged with people, mostly tourists, jostling each other as they walked in opposite directions, yet never, in the forty-plus years he had lived in York, had he heard of anyone falling off the unguarded wall on to the grassy bank. The fall was unlikely to be fatal, even injurious, unless one was frail, elderly, but the possibility of such an accident was real and constant, yet in Hennessey's observation, it never seemed to happen. That particular walk was tinged with an unexpected sadness in that he noticed, for the first time, that the original railway station, which had survived within the walls in use as a warehouse, had been evidently quickly and speedily demolished even though Hennessey would have thought it merited the status of a listed building, and a new office block built on the site. The new building, in brown brick, was low-rise and blended neatly, not at all threatening the Minster for dominance of the city, yet the absence of the old station caused Hennessey to feel an unexpected sense of loss. He glanced to his left, and looked beyond the present railway station, to the terraces of YO26, uniformly drab and huddled together. If those houses were human beings, he thought, they would be second-class passengers in a crowded railway train elbowing and apologizing to each other, whilst in the vehicles nearer the engine in the same train, the first-class passengers each had a seat to themselves, with spare seating available.

He walked on and pondered his conversation with Commander Sharkey. Appearance and reality, he thought, as he glanced up at the sky, still blue with five-tenths cloud and now a warm wind blowing. Appearance and reality. The commander had once again been troubled by the death of 'Johnny' Taighe, a maths teacher, who was close to retirement, smoked like a chimney, tippled heavily in the evening – his bulbous red nose said so – who had entered teaching via the ex-serviceman's one-year crash course. He had survived teaching lower-school maths for all his working life, and when he should have been allowed to soft-pedal towards retirement, he was given final-year maths to teach to national exams. 'He didn't even know what "interpolation" meant, George,' the commander had said in a plaintive, appealing tone, as if asking for mercy, or alms, or both. 'He was burnt out and out of his depth. He was giving off all the danger signals, the heavy smoking, the false good humour . . . none of the other staff picked up on it, and they were all, oh, so surprised when he keeled over with a massive coronary. Dead before he hit the ground, at home in front of his wife.' The commander had paused. 'For many years I was pleased for him that he escaped the indignity of croaking in the corridor, or in front of class, but I have subsequently found out that if you work for the local authority, your next of kin is entitled to a handsome, one-off payment if you should die at your place of work, or in pursuit of your employment, if away from your actual place of work. Looking back, Johnny wasn't a wealthy man and, I dare say, his family would have noticed the benefit if his ticker had stopped just an hour or two earlier . . . but what I am building up to saying—' Hennessey had then cut him off – with a raised hand and a smile, he assured the commander that he was 'fine', that he was 'fit and well', he was not 'burned out', nor was he out of his depth like the unfortunate Johnny Taighe, he did not want to 'soft-pedal' towards retirement by policing his desk.

'So long as you know that if it gets too pressured, George,' the commander had smiled. 'I was fifteen or sixteen years old when Johnny Taighe died so tragically short of a deserved retirement, and so I don't feel in any way responsible, but the incident reached me in later life and I am determined that it won't happen to one of mine. So long as you're clear about that, George?'

'Perfectly, thank you, Commander.' Hennessey had then made to rise and the commander had asked him to 'wait a minute, please'. Hennessey had sat resignedly and had hoped that his facial expression and body language conveyed to the commander that he was 'waiting a minute' under protest. If said facial expression and body language was observed by the commander then he was clearly not influenced by it, because he had leant forward and grimaced and by doing so, transmitted to Hennessey that this was going to be a particularly long 'minute' to be waited. Hennessey had known what was coming, and it came: 'I'm worried about corruption in the nick, George,' he had then said, in tones of clear anguish. And it transpired to be the tale that Commander Sharkey had told so often before, of his time in the Royal Hong Kong Police, about which he made the courageous and, dangerous to his career, admission that he had taken bribes. 'Sort of negative corruption, you see, George. It wasn't corruption like the corruption we mean in the UK – didn't tamper with evidence or anything . . . it was in the manner of being told not to take a patrol into a specified district on a specified night, or sometimes told not to come into work that day at all, and if I complied there would be a brown envelope of readies in my desk drawer the next morning. But if I hadn't complied . . . well, a one-way trip to the Forbidden City . . . or a swim with the blue dolphins.' Hennessey had, as so often before, said, 'I quite understand, sir.'

'Got out quick, only there for a few months, weeks in fact, but I was there and I have been contaminated with that corruption . . . and that's for me to deal with. But I am terrified of corruption in this nick. I have seen how insidious it is . . . like a worm inside an apple. Once an officer has been corrupted, even against his better judgement, it's impossible to uncorrupt him and still have him in the force.'

'I am sure I would have heard of something, sir,' Hennessey had tried to placate Sharkey.

'But, you don't see . . .' Sharkey had held his head in his hands. 'That's the nature of the beast, you don't know it's there until it is manifest and manifest in a large and positive way.'

Hennessey had managed to extricate himself from the emotional clutches of the commander within an hour of being summoned to his office, and had left the police station to walk to York City Hospital, to the pathology laboratory, to Dr D'Acre and the mortuary attendant, the bubbly, effervescent Eric Filey. He turned away from looking across the tracks at the black roofs of Holgate and looked at the ribbon of wall ahead of him. He pondered the commander, he pondered how a man whose appearance was so immaculate could have a mind in such turmoil.

Appearance and reality.

Four

In which a suspect is quizzed and George Hennessey is at home to the gracious reader.

'It gives her age at death as being twenty years, plus or minus twelve months.' Louise D'Acre sat in her small and cramped office adjacent to the pathology laboratory. She scanned the report, focusing on the paper and not allowing George Hennessey any eye contact at all.

'Well, that's good news and bad news.' He forced a smile.

'Oh?'

'Yes . . . you see the age range of the mis pers we suspect to be the victims are aged between nineteen and twenty-one . . . so one is not highlighted by that information, but because the age of death is what you say it is, it means we are not looking for a fifth victim.'

'We have the lower dentures, in diagram form that is, they show dental work, British dental work . . . they were all British girls?'

'Yes . . . all English . . . at least they all had home addresses in England.'

'Well, if any of their dentists keep records from twenty years ago, you could make a match. She was quite a short girl, about five foot three inches in height, one hundred and fifty six or seven centimetres.'

'That ought to narrow it down,' Hennessey said, smiling, grateful for any knowledge or insight that the doctor could offer.

'That's an approximation, you understand?' Dr D'Acre's voice was calm, controlled, detailed. 'We have to add up to two inches or five centimetres on to the length of the skeleton to come to an approximation of the deceased person's height in life. This is to allow for the fleshy pad on the sole of the feet and for cartilage shrinkage, which pulls the bones together at the joints, the hips and knees especially.'

'I see.'

'So allowing for that, the first skeleton to be examined in this case was about 5' 3" tall, or 156/7 centimetres, if you prefer the metric measurement. No trace of poisons in the long bones. If she had been poisoned by heavy poisons such as arsenic, it would still be present but it's absent as is any other heavy poison, such as cyanide, but lighter poisons, opium, carbon monoxide, would leave no trace after this length of time. I didn't expect to find poison traces, but it pays to be thorough. Horrible death though.'

'Awful . . .' Hennessey pondered the victim, being dragged naked to her death across rough ground, thrown into a pit and her skull smashed with a spade and all the while carrying a little something in her mouth which she was leaving for the police, to help them trace her killers. Plucky isn't the word, he thought, neither is selflessness . . . nor clarity of thought when all hope must have been lost. Truly awful.

'Well.' Dr D'Acre stood. 'Since you have arrived, shall we look at the other three?'

Hennessey followed her out of the office mumbling his apologies and explaining that his commander had wanted to talk about 'a pressing matter'. It was, he thought, not a matter that had not also been equally pressing twelve months ago, and would probably be equally pressing in twelve months' time. Dr D'Acre went to the female changing room, Hennessey to the male and having donned lightweight green coveralls, plus hats, they met outside the pathology laboratory and entered.

'Afternoon, doctor. Afternoon, sir.' The rotund Eric Filey beamed as Dr D'Acre and George Hennessey entered the laboratory.

'Afternoon, Mr Filey.' D'Acre smiled briefly.

'Afternoon.' Hennessey walked to his place, as observing police officer, at the very edge of the room. Protocol dictated that he should not approach the dissecting table unless invited to do so by the pathologist. The room he found, as always, smelled strongly of formaldehyde and had five stainless-steel tables arranged in a row with generous working space between each table. The tables were supported on single, circular columns and had 'lips' of approximately, guessed Hennessey, two inches around the edge. Quite sufficient to prevent the flow of blood from a corpse spilling on to the floor, allowing it to drain away through the plug hole and down the centre of the column that supported each table. The pathology laboratory was enclosed by four walls and lighted by artificial light only, powerful filament bulbs shimmering brilliantly behind perspex covers. On that afternoon, three of the five tables contained the skeletonized remains of human beings, each lying face up, each grinning at the ceiling with fully exposed teeth and hollows in the skull where once their eyes had been.

'Skeleton one.' Dr D'Acre adjusted the microphone above the table, which was attached to a stainless-steel anglepoise arm, which in turn was attached to the ceiling.

It was a small, neat device, not at all clearly visible on the arm, but it was there, and powerful, well able to pick up even the most soft-spoken of commentaries. 'File number LD/9/27/01/09 of my records.' She turned and smiled at Hennessey. 'Just means this is the twenty-seventh post-mortem I have done this month.'

'Ah . . .' Hennessey nodded.

'I'll attach a name to the file as soon as you can provide one.'

'Of course.'

'The corpse is female, completely skeletonized.' Dr D'Acre spoke for the benefit of the microphone. 'It's . . . Can you assist, please, Mr Filey?' She took a metal tape measure from the tray of instruments beside her and extended it from skull to foot of the skeleton, '. . . approximately six feet in length . . . or 180 centimetres. A tall young woman in life . . . immediately obvious is a crush fracture to the skull. As with the first skeleton to be examined in this case, consistent with being struck from behind with the flat of a spade blade. Death would have been instantaneous. No other injuries . . . but . . . no, this could help in her identification. Mr Hennessey, she has a healed fracture of her left tibia and . . . a healed fracture of her left femur.'

'Sorry . . . her tibia and femur?'

'Shin bone and thigh bone respectively. She broke the left leg in two places, the fractures look about the same age. Sustained not too long before she died . . . not childhood injuries. Perhaps a year or two before she was murdered, she broke her left leg in an accident.'

'In two places,' Hennessey echoed.

'In two places. They have been reset, so she was hospitalized rapidly. She didn't drag herself across the

79

tundra for weeks on end with a broken leg, she was close to medical facilities when it happened.'

'Good, good, that's a little bit of personal history we can use to help identify her,' Hennessey said. 'Every bit counts.'

'Oh, yes, identification has been confirmed by the minutest of details before now.' Dr D'Acre prised open the jaw of the skeleton. Hennessey winced as the jaws 'gave' with a loud crack. He had heard the sound often before, but it still affected him. 'Well, again, dental work, British dentistry. Something else to aid the identification and no other indications of cause of death.' Dr D'Acre stepped back from the stainless-steel table, and glanced at Hennessey. 'Same as before, head bashed in with a heavy, flat object.'

'What's the betting it will be the same with the other two?'

'I am not a betting lady, Chief Inspector, but if I were . . . well, I wouldn't bet against it.'

'Neither would I.'

Dr D'Acre walked to the next table and examined the skull. 'Yes –' she nodded – 'I would have been wise not to have bet against it.' She moved on to the fourth skeleton. 'Again, same injury.'

'Four young women,' Hennessey mused aloud, 'each battered over the head with a heavy, flat instrument, and buried in a shallow grave.'

'In the same field.' Dr D'Acre prised open the mouth of the third skeleton. 'Again, British dentistry and no "little present" for you.' She returned to the second skeleton and examined the mouth and reported British dentistry and also no 'present' left for the police. 'Did you find anything out about the old house that stood on the land? I meant to ask you.' She examined the limbs of the third skeleton.

'Yes, in fact DS Yellich obtained an interesting history,' and Hennessey proceeded to tell Dr D'Acre about the dysfunctional and inappropriately named Smiley family who seemed to have done anything but smile.

'I was right . . .' Louise D'Acre, by contrast, allowed herself a rare smile and the briefest of eye contact with George Hennessey. 'That house did have an atmosphere. I knew I felt something.'

'Not from the crime that went on there, perhaps?' Hennessey had in his life felt a 'presence' in not a few places. His interest in military history had led him to walk many battlefields over the years, though he had felt a presence on only one, that one being Gettysburg in Virginia. He would not, he often said, want to spend a night on Gettysburg field. And because of his experiences, walking into an alley and thinking and feeling 'something happened', or into a house and thinking and feeling the same thing, he would not dismiss anybody who said that a room or a house had an atmosphere. If he didn't feel any such atmosphere, he was quite prepared to concede that that didn't mean there was no presence. It meant only that he didn't feel it.

'No . . . in my experience, such atmosphere comes either from violent death – but these women met their deaths away from the house – or a prolonged, dys-functional family can leave a similar atmosphere, so I believe. I sensed great unhappiness in that house, not violent death.'

'It seems you were right.'

'The girls' fear would have been relatively short-lived.' Dr D'Acre took a tape measure and measured the third skeleton. 'A long time for them, each day must have seemed as long as a year, if they were kept there at all. Those notches in the skirting board may be totally

81

irrelevant, though somehow I don't think they are . . . though here I wander into your territory.'

'Oh, wander all you like, Dr D'Acre, wander all you like. But I would agree with you, I don't think they are irrelevant. I think they're quite the opposite. That chain . . . that padlock . . .'

'Makes you shudder . . . skeleton number two is five feet four inches in length, possibly a woman of five-five or five-six in life, or about one hundred and sixty-two centimetres. She has no other injuries of any type or age upon her skeleton.'

'I see.'

'But equally –' Dr D'Acre moved round the table to the third skeleton, carrying the tape measure with her – 'some houses have a pleasant atmosphere. My first house, for example, was a small cottage in the Vale that had a tranquillity about it, which I am sure was the legacy of a couple who had lived there for forty years before I moved in. It must have been a most successful marriage and I am pleased for them in the way they died, both together in a car accident. I think they would have wanted it like that. If they had died separately, one before the other, the remaining partner would just have pined away . . . but the feeling of peace they left behind in their house was so strong that it remained after my burglary . . . and the burglars wrecked the place . . . still the tranquillity survived and that helped me deal with the trauma of the burglary . . . and skeleton number three is five feet six inches in length, giving a lifetime height of about five feet seven inches or about one hundred and sixty-seven centimetres. She also has no other injuries, save for previously observed, and likely cause of death, massively fractured skull.'

'Thanks . . . we can move forward with that. If the

heights you have provided us with tie in with the heights given on the mis per sheets, it'll be enough for us to call on some families with good news or bad news depending on how you look at it.'

'Good news?' Dr D'Acre raised an eyebrow.

'In my experience, families who have had members go missing and remain missing for years are relieved that the awful sense of unknowing has ended, a body they can lay to rest, a grave they can visit . . .'

'Yes . . . I can understand that. Oh . . . if one of my children should go missing, and I didn't know what had happened to them . . . oh my.'

'Well, if we can match the remains with missing persons, the case ought to begin to unravel.'

'You hope.'

'I hope, but I think it will. The tall girl, with the broken leg and arm . . . that sounds promising, we could be making a match there. Six feet is tall for a woman, not many six-foot-tall women will have been reported missing when in their twenties, who, recent to their disappearance, had once broken their leg in two places.'

'And done so simultaneously,' Dr D'Acre added. 'I'll have the medical photographer photograph the skulls so that the photograph of the skull might be superimposed on any photographs taken of the victims in life. Even without the lower jaw that would still be possible, but I'll leave the jaw on these three until after the photographs have been taken.'

'Thanks.'

'They are all Caucasian, or white European, by the way . . .'

'As are the four mis pers we think that they might be.'

'I'll run a trace for heavy poisons as a matter of

course, and I'll extract a tooth from each to give an age at death plus or minus one year. Full report will be faxed as soon as possible. For your attention, Chief Inspector?'

'Yes, please, but that's enough to be working on for the time being. More than enough in fact.'

'Took over from Mr Forester. He left us a very healthy concern, the price we paid was fair and reasonable. He will have no money troubles for the rest of his life, unless he squanders it.'

'Which has been known.' Yellich read the office in which he sat – spacious, airy, massive windows, huge sheets of glass on two sides, plaster walls painted with a pastel lilac shade, decorated with Impressionist prints. The man to whom he talked sat behind a 'space-age' desk of light alloy, atop which was a battery of three phones, one white, one red, one black. The nameplate on the desk said, Dalton, Managing Director. Dalton in person was trim, neatly dressed, a flash of gold when he smiled, which matched the gold tie pin and gold-coloured clip of the ballpoint or pen which showed in the breast pocket of his jacket.

'Which indeed does happen, but not, I think, to Tom Forester. I know him and like him. He's a Yorkshireman, as shrewd as they come, wouldn't know it to speak to him, warm, friendly manner, but a brain as sharp as a tack when it comes to business. You've met him?'

'Yesterday.'

'I see, and he sent you here?'

'No . . . he didn't send me anywhere, but gave information which led the police here.'

'I see . . . sorry.'

'Can I ask, do you use the same cleaning company that

Mr Forester used when he was the owner and managing director of this company?'

'I believe so . . .' Dalton was clearly puzzled by the question. 'I am sure we do, in fact – we haven't changed cleaners since we took over from Mr Forester, and so the answer is likely to be "yes". An outfit called Steps and Stairs. Arrive in a yellow van, all dressed in light blue tracksuits . . . they look smart, are quite efficient and their costs are reasonable.'

'Do you have their contact number?'

'Easily obtainable for you, if you'd like it.'

'I would, please, and if you have it, the number of the gardening service called Ace of Spades? That's if you still use them?'

'Again, yes we do.' Dalton pressed an intercom on the desk and said, 'Susie, can you get me the number of Steps and Stairs and Ace of Spades? Thank you.' He released the switch. He smiled at Yellich. 'You want more than that, Mr Yellich?'

'I do.' Yellich returned the smile.

'The numbers of these small service companies are easily obtained in the Yellow Pages.'

'Yes . . . clutching at a straw really, Mr Dalton, but you are correct . . . it's a question of promotional pens with the company name on them, small, black, like a bookie's ballpoint.'

Dalton opened a drawer in his desk and took out a pen. Yellich saw it was identical to the pen taken from the mouth of the first skeleton to be unearthed. 'Like this?'

'Like that indeed.' Yellich reached forward and took it from Dalton's hand when Dalton offered it. 'Yes, like this indeed. Do you mind if I hang on to this?'

'Be my guest. It's the last pen of a batch ordered by Mr Forester; he was a little embarrassed about them.'

'Yes –' Yellich smiled – 'he told me.'

'Can't give them to business contacts, ended up giving them to employees and cleaners and the like to take home to their children. He took a batch of a couple of hundred and there just were not that many employees and gardeners and cleaners to hand them out to and so many remained and they have trickled out of the company over the last twenty years. That one is one of the few that remains . . .'

The door of Dalton's office opened with a gentle click. A young, lemon-haired woman in a yellow dress entered and handed Dalton a small piece of paper. 'The numbers you wanted, Mr Dalton.'

'Thank you, Susie.' Dalton took the sheet of paper and Susie turned on her heels and walked out of the office. 'Here you are.' Dalton handed the telephone numbers to Yellich. Yellich glanced at them and clipped them in his notepad.

'Can you say precisely when you took over the company, Mr Dalton?'

'Just over twenty years ago.'

'I see, and you continued Mr Forester's practice of giving the pens away to sundry folk who have some loose affiliation with the company?'

'Well . . . yes.'

Yellich searched his memory, the first disappearance and the last straddled the taking over of the company by Dalton from Forester. If Michael Henderson was confused about the date, even though his memory had proved accurate as to the location, then he could have witnessed the girl being murdered after Dalton took over the company. The pen in her mouth could have come from Dalton's hand, as easily as it could have come from Forester's. 'Can I ask you, Mr Dalton, when you were newly the MD of this company, do you recall giving the pens to anyone in particular, either in ones or twos or in a handful? Anyone at all?'

'Whether associated with the company or not?'

'Anyone, in any capacity?'

'Well . . . this is going back some way, but I remember the "new days" as I call them . . . doubtless you remember your first day on the beat with more clarity than you remember any given day last week.'

'I do, actually . . . I don't remember yesterday well.'

'It's a sign of being busy . . . well I gave some to my own children . . . and their friends. Doubt if you're interested in them?'

'Doubt it too.'

'Police inquiries . . . would it be fair to assume that you are asking if I can identify a recipient of one such pen who might be of criminal intent?'

'It would be fair.'

'Yes . . . actually, though I didn't exactly give the pen away. And only now recall the incident. At the time I took over the company, my wife used to run a small car, a Citroën 2CV . . . ingenious design, no longer in production, but the design was, as I said, ingenious. Even began to break down my entrenched Francophobia, but it was repaired once by a man who offered to visit people at home so as to repair their cars in the garage of the owner. Had a massive van, full of spare parts, specialized in Citroëns – "Citroën Repairs at Home". So we gave him a go when the brakes became faulty and the car was clearly going to fail its annual roadworthiness test. Fellow by the name of Pinder. He turned up when he said he would, did the job well enough and his fee was about what he quoted. I wrote him a cheque, actually using one of the pens, and he asked to borrow the pen to scribble the receipt. Having done so, he pocketed the pen and just turned and walked away. I wasn't really bothered, I thought it was a piece of forgetfulness on his part and the pens were there to be given away anyway, though I did think it was a bit rude. But that night I was lying in my bed next to my wife and she suddenly reached across and grabbed my groin and said, "That man is not coming here again." '

'Oh?'

'The accumulation of many things . . . that when he asked to use the toilet my wife knew he went into more rooms than just the bathroom, that he looked at our daughter, who was about ten at the time, in a very unhealthy way, my wife said, anyway, and of course I believed her. My wife also said that she felt she was being "sucked in" by him, as though he could make her do things she knew were wrong but she'd do them anyway. She said that he was "getting inside her head", was the expression she used, by means of eye contact and a very intense way of speaking. Children wouldn't be able to resist him. So my wife said.'

'Pinder, you say?'

'Yes. Can't remember his first name, but I have seen his van about the Vale, so he's still in business, still in the Vale. Small man. Very small.'

'Sucked in?' Hennessey raised an eyebrow.

'That's what he said his wife said, boss.' Yellich cradled the half-drunk mug of coffee in his hands and leaned back in his chair. 'He's got previous for theft, but nothing really heavy.'

'Mind you, I think I know what he meant . . .' Hennessey glanced out of the small window of his office at the wall, by then basking in late afternoon sun. A little, and last, vestige of the summer before the winter set in, he fancied. 'I have met such people, they are adept at playing what I believe have come to be called "mind games". In my youth we just said they were downright manipulative, but whatever, such men are dangerous, especially to women and children. Sounds like we ought to quiz him. I think that's a two-hander. If he's a game player, it'll be a two-hander.'

'I think you're right, boss. Anything come of the post-mortems?'

'Nothing,' said Hennessey, 'that was unexpected, that is . . . all died in the same way, smashed on the back of the head with a wide, heavy object.'

'The blade of a spade?'

'Has to be . . . all apparently naked when they died, no metal was found around the bones in the form of zip fasteners or bra clips, or key rings or such like. Dr D'Acre was able to assess the height in life and saw that one of the skeletons had sustained a previous injury, fractured her left leg in two places.'

'That'll help with the ID.'

'Certainly will. She was a tall girl, six feet tall in life. And that is the height given as being Melita Campion's height in life. She being one of the four women reported to be missing in the period in question. Family home in the Smoke. Greenwich, no less.'

Yellich smiled. 'Paying a home visit, boss?'

Hennessey returned the smile. 'Well, each family home will have to be visited if only to eliminate the possibility that the women had any link other than an address in Holgate and that they were all students, but I will go and visit her home address. I have a personal interest.'

'It's good to return and walk your roots from time to time, skipper.'

'If I have time I will do so, depends where in Greenwich they are, but if I am travelling from York, well, I'll find time, even if I have to do it in a single day. But to matters in hand, Mr Pinder . . . ?'

'Repairs at home.'

'I'd like to quiz him sooner rather than later.' Hennessey turned in his chair and reached for the *Yellow Pages* and looked up 'Car Repairs'. '"Pinder's Repairs at Home" . . . well, he's still in business, as your informant says. Not doing too well though, lives in Clementhorpe. Some lovely, decent salt-of-the-earth types in Clementhorpe, but no lottery winners, that's for sure. Come on, we'll pay him a call.'

Jeffrey Pinder sat on a PVC-covered settee and scowled at Yellich and Hennessey. He gave little away in terms of body movement but his eyes were deep-set and staring. The front room of his council house was cluttered and unclean, the carpet stuck to the soles of the officers' shoes, the windows were grimy but through them could be seen Pinder's van, parked half on, half off the kerb. He was a stocky man, with stubby fingers, matted hair. By 4.15 p.m. he was still dressed in pyjamas and dressing gown and carpet slippers. Hennessey asked if he was unwell.

'No.' Pinder snarled the reply. His voice was soft but his accent was strong. 'Only get dressed if I go out. Business is slow. Slow. Slow.'

'Slow?'

Pinder tossed a thumb towards the window. 'See that van out there, that van hasn't moved in two weeks. That's slow for a self-employed man that survives from one job to the next, that is slow.' Pinder's voice, too, remained slow; but his eyes continued to search Hennessey's. When he invited the officers to sit down and both declined, Hennessey saw Pinder's eyes narrow in surprise or annoyance, or both. He was clearly a man who liked to control people. Dangerous indeed.

'How old are you, Mr Pinder?'

'Fifty-five. Just turned.'

'And you've been self-employed for all your working life?'

'Most of it. Started out working for a bloke but didn't like being told what to do, so I went out on my own. More hassle but I like the freedom.'

'When did you start out on your own?'

'About twenty years ago.'

'Who did you work for before you went out on your own?'

'Few folk. Always in the motor trade.'

'Ever work for Mallard's?' Yellich asked, suddenly, spontaneously.

'Yes.'

Yellich's heart thumped, beside him he felt Hennessey stiffen.

'Why, is it a crime?'

'Nope . . . just interesting.' Hennessey glanced round the room. Discarded metal foil takeaway cartons spoke of a single existence. Flies buzzed in numbers that Hennessey wouldn't have tolerated.

'In what way?'

'In a very interesting way,' Yellich said and, reading Hennessey's mind, he asked, 'Are you a bachelor?'

'Yes . . . can't you tell . . . if I had a woman I wouldn't be living in a tip like this. I'd have her clean up around me.'

'I imagine you would.'

'I am not ashamed of how I live. I didn't get the breaks that other people got. That's not a crime either.'

'So, when did you quit Mallard's?'

'Last job I had. About twenty years ago.'

'What did you do for them?'

'Fitter . . . motor mechanic to you.'

'I know what a fitter is, thank you.'

'At the York depot?'

'Wherever a car needed repairing, York, Selby.'

'Anywhere else?'

'Nope. Not for Mallard's. They didn't have anywhere else. Just garages in York and Selby.'

'I see. I understand you once did a job for a Mr Dalton.'

'Did I?'

'Yes.'

'If you say so . . . I don't keep records . . . prefer cash in hand, less bother. All that fiddly paperwork, I like to avoid that.'

'All the fiddly income tax . . . bet you like to avoid that as well.'

Pinder remained silent, but his eyes burned into Hennessey's.

'You took a pen from him,' Yellich said.

'Did I?'

'He says you did.'

'How long ago was this?'

'Twenty years ago, possibly less.'

Pinder's mouth curled into a smirk. 'You honestly expect me to remember what I did twenty years ago?'

'If it's significant.'

'Well I don't, mate. I don't remember a fella called . . . whatever. Dalton did you say? I don't remember him.'

'He had a daughter. About ten at the time.'

Pinder's eyes narrowed again. That observation had struck a chord. Hennessey thought he looked worried. 'Remember a little girl, and a house in which you went walkabout when you wished to use the bathroom?'

Pinder remained silent.

'Remember now?'

'I'm saying nothing.'

'Why?' Hennessey asked.

'Got something to hide?' Yellich prompted.

Pinder remained silent.

'Mind if we take a look around your house?'

'And in your van?'

'Yes.' Pinder tensed. 'Yes, I mind. You have a warrant?'

'Know the law, do you, Mr Pinder?' Yellich asked. 'Mind you, the answer's yes. I checked with criminal records . . . you came across as being a bit light fingered.'

'That was a long time ago.'

'The last conviction doesn't mean the last offence . . . it means the last time you were found out.'

'Nothing worth nicking in the Dalton household?'

'I don't remember the Dalton household.'

'Or a small black pen, like the ones bookies use?'

'I don't do paperwork. What do I need a pen for?'

'Don't know, what do you need a pen for?' Yellich pressed but received no reply.

'Have you any mates, Mr Pinder?'

'Few. Down the pub.'

'Had you a mate twenty years ago?'

'Dare say . . . always had mates . . . now, twenty years ago . . .'

'A guy . . . about as big as you?'

'Possibly.'

'So you don't mind if we look around?'

'Yes I mind.'

'Why, what are we going to find?'

'Nothing that shouldn't be here.'

'Really, so why do you mind?'

'I'm not proud of how I live.'

Hennessey nodded. 'Listen, we are experienced police officers, we have seen it all and we're not making judgements about anybody's living conditions.'

'You'll still need a warrant.'

'It'll take me half an hour to get one. Meanwhile Detective Sergeant Yellich here will stay in the house, to make sure nothing . . . and nobody, leaves. And when I return I'll bring a team of constables with me and we'll tear the place apart.'

'But if you give us your permission to look around,' Yellich added with a smile, 'we'll be very, very, ever so, really thoughtfully careful.'

'Promise.' Hennessey smiled.

'How did you find me?' Pinder sat forward and held his head in his hands.

'Just good, old-fashioned detective work,' Hennessey said after he and Yellich glanced at each other with raised eyebrows.

'And I thought I'd covered me tracks.'

'Nobody ever covers their tracks fully, Jeffrey. Not even old-school felons like you.'

'Guy's got to live . . . work wasn't coming in, I suppose in the pokey I'll get a varied diet. I was getting fed up with chicken chow mein from the takeaway, and a wash too, I'll get that.'

'A bath at least once a week.'

'So, where is it?'

'Front bedroom.'

Hennessey had probably 'seen it all' but even with his

eye of a very experienced police officer, he was more than a little surprised at Pinder's 'bedroom'; behind him Yellich, with less experience, gasped.

There was no bed, that was what Hennessey and Yellich had both been struck by, they found, when they later talked about it. The bedroom was just a jumble of cushions and sheets. It was clear that when Jeffrey Pinder wanted to sleep, he fell on to the pile of cushions, squirmed around until he got comfortable, pulled the sheet over him and let sleep take him. Empty cans, many empty cans, of super-strength lager lying on the floor and among the cushions attested to the manner in which Pinder invited sleep. Opposite the pile of cushions was a wardrobe. Hennessey opened it gingerly. He surveyed the contents and said, 'Well, well, well.'

'What is it, boss?' Yellich tried to crane his neck round the door of the wardrobe.

'Take a butcher's.' Hennessey stepped further into the room, thus allowing Yellich to view the interior of the wardrobe.

'A dressing-up box.' Yellich viewed the clothing, hanging there, all female clothing, and on the shelves within the wardrobe were items of jewellery, brooches, watches, again; all female. 'But not in itself criminal,' he added, 'depending on how they were acquired.'

'He feels guilty about something though, something he thinks will invite a stretch in the slammer.'

'Still, guilt doesn't necessarily mean criminality . . . I mean, I feel guilty about things I've done that are not even remotely criminal.'

Hennessey sifted through the clothing on the hangers, came to a white blouse with frilly cuffs and paused. He lifted the collar above the hanger and said, 'I think, in this case, he has reason to worry . . . read that name.'

'Melita Campion,' Yellich said with a draw of breath. 'Bingo, boss, bingo, bingo, bingo.'

'Better get Scenes of Crime here: we have to take this house apart, and the van too. Though it won't be the same van used to abduct them, but it might contain something.'

'Very good, boss, and Pinder?'

'Arrest him on suspicion of murder. Arrange for the van to be taken to Wetherby.'

'I don't know, I don't remember where I got the blouse.' Pinder sat forwards, resting his elbows on the table.

'You like women's clothing?'

'Yes. So what? I like their flimsiness. It does something for me.'

'So where did you get that blouse?' Hennessey leaned forwards. The third person in the room, a frail-looking, slightly built man with silver hair who had introduced himself, 'for the tape', as Stanley Benson, of Benson, Hardwick and Benson, solicitors, remained silent, though clearly listening with total concentration.

'Where I get most of my clothing from.'

'Where is that?'

'Charity shops.'

Hennessey paused. 'Charity shops?'

'I don't care what they think. Sad old guy that buys women's clothes . . . the sales women snigger at me, but so what? Sometimes I steal them from washing lines. OK, that's theft, but I haven't done that for a while . . . too old now.'

It was a fair point, Hennessey had to concede that. Stealing clothing from washing lines was a young person's crime. Jeffrey Pinder was not a young person, and was not even a fit person for his years. Takeaway Chinese meals and super-strength lager had clearly taken its toll on whatever health he retained as he edged into his fifties and towards his sixties.

'What about the jewellery?'

'What about it?'

'Where did it come from?'

'Here and there.'

'Some nice items amongst them. Don't get such like from charity shops.'

'Don't you?' Pinder's eyes showed life in the way they had shown life before, deeply searching Hennessey's eyes. 'I have done, once or twice, found a brass brooch in a wicker basket, any item for a pound, it said. But it was too elaborate to be brass, too much delicate working, took it home, polished it up.'

'Gold?'

'Yes . . . sold it for a very nice profit.'

'I bet you did, but such finds in charity shops are too rare to account for all the jewellery in the wardrobe. In excess of forty items.'

Pinder shrugged his shoulders.

'Tell me something, Mr Pinder –' Hennessey sat back in his chair and continued to avoid eye contact with Pinder – 'what else are we going to find in your house?' Then he looked up and saw Pinder's eyes narrow. He'd struck a chord.

'You're searching the house?'

'Yes. As we speak. We have your permission. Remember?'

'But you found the clothes and the jewellery . . . what more do you want?'

'Whatever it is you don't want us to find. We'll dig up the garden if we have to.'

Pinder glanced at Hennessey. Hennessey knew that he had struck yet another chord.

'Like burying things, do you, Mr Pinder?'

'No comment.'

'How long have you had the tenancy of that property?'

'No comment.'

'We can find out.'

'Can I ask what is your line of questioning, Mr Hennessey?' Benson spoke for the first time and revealed an educated voice with a softened Yorkshire accent. 'You do seem to be beating around the bush, and I am getting confused. I am sure Mr Pinder is also getting confused.'

'You could say that again.' Pinder scowled at Hennessey.

'Very well, Mr Pinder. You will be detained in custody tonight, to appear before York City magistrates tomorrow, in which hearing we will ask for permission to detain you for a further seven days to assist us with our enquiries.'

'In connection with what?' Benson directed his question at Hennessey. 'I really have to insist you be more specific, Chief Inspector.'

'If you had not been detained, Mr Pinder,' Hennessey continued, ignoring Benson, 'you would have returned home and switched on the six p.m. news.'

'I don't watch the news.'

'Really? Well, if you did and if you watched the regional news you would have seen an item about four bodies having been recovered from an area of waste ground . . . quite a remote location between York and Selby.'

'So?'

'The bodies, skeletons really, are of four young women who disappeared a number of years ago.'

'So?'

'One of the women was called Melita Campion . . . whose blouse was found hanging in your wardrobe.'

'Know nothing about that . . .'

'You don't help yourself by lying, Mr Pinder.'

'I'm not lying.'

'You said you'd never been near Mallard's depot.'

'You were sacked from Mallard's for stealing from their cars, in their depot.'

Pinder remained silent.

'Just a phone call, that's all it took, just before I came here. That's why you went self-employed. Couldn't get a job with anyone after being sacked for stealing from your employers. The bodies were found in the field next to Mallard's depot. So you knew the field existed. It's so remote, you'd have to know it existed, and you'd have to know the property on the field was derelict, at least abandoned, because that's where you kept them for days on end before you and your mate frog-marched them to a hole in the ground, whacked them over the head with a spade and buried them.'

Benson glanced worriedly at Pinder.

'And if one item of jewellery can be identified as belonging to any one of the victims . . . well in that case, things won't look good for you. Won't look good at all. So make it easy for yourself or make it hard.'

Pinder glared at Hennessey.

Silence. The twin tapes spun, the red recording light glowed.

'So, who's your mate?' Hennessey pressed.

Before Pinder answered there was a knock on the door. Yellich entered.

'DS Yellich has entered the room at 1806 hours,' Hennessey said as procedure dictated, all in accordance with the Police and Criminal Evidence Act 1985.

'A word, boss.' Yellich smiled at Hennessey.

'The interview is halted at 1806 hours.' Hennessey switched off the tape and stood. 'You might want to make use of this time to take a bit of legal advice, Mr Pinder,' Hennessey added, then left the room to join Yellich in the corridor.

'News?' Hennessey put a coin in the hot drinks vending machine. He selected tea, no sugar.

'Goldmine, boss.' Yellich beamed. 'The house is an Aladdin's cave.'

'Really?'

'Really, but only low-grade stuff in the main: inexpensive watches, although countless numbers of same, cheap jewellery, VCRs, camcorders . . .'

'Proceeds of burglaries?'

'I'd say. The boy's a fence, he's clearly been receiving stolen goods, enough to charge him and detain him without going to the magistrate for a warrant to detain.'

'Look in the van?'

'Yes, boss, nothing out of the ordinary, fitted out with shelves and the shelves are full of bits of Citroën and tools, and a girlie calendar without which the motor trade is incomplete. Mind you, Miss September is really quite nice.'

'Mind on the job, Yellich,' but said with a smile. 'Did you look in the garden?'

'Glanced at it – just a normal, overgrown, postage-stamp-sized council house garden. House had a brick-built outbuilding, nothing in there that looked out of place. Found this though . . .' Yellich dipped his hand into his inside pocket and took out a building society passbook which had, by then, been placed in a cellophane productions bag. 'It's in the name of James Payne, and contains quite a lot of money.'

'Quite a lot? How much is that? What I think is quite a lot would not be what a Kuwaiti oil sheikh would call a lot.'

'A hundred thousand pounds, sir. In excess of.'

'Well, from our perspective, that's a lot. You think it's been stolen?'

'At first, yes, sir, I did. But even if an inexperienced house-breaker would pick it up, a fence wouldn't want to keep it. Can't do anything with it, unless you are James Payne. All that passbook is, is a little book with a lot of figures in it. So why keep it?'

'Why indeed?' Hennessey tapped the book. 'James Payne, Jeffrey Pinder . . . J.P.'

'I noticed that too, boss.'

'A double life, you think?'

'It's been known, but if you have that sort of money, why live in squalor and make a living as a jobbing mechanic?'

'Again, why indeed.' Hennessey paused. 'Alright. Have you left a constable at the scene?'

'Yes, sir.'

'Good. You've done enough for one day, we're both into overtime now . . . it's the way of police work . . . as you well know by now. Can you arrange for a constable to be posted on the house all night?'

'Yes, sir. I'll leave a note for the night shift, have him relieved at ten p.m. He's a young lad and was already clearly nervous at being left on his own, but he's safe, the estate isn't Indian country. It'll do him good to learn he can survive without his mates around him.'

'Yes, we all had to stand a lonely watch for the first time, and now they all have personal radios. All I had when I was a young copper was a whistle and if that got knocked out of your hand, you really were on your own.

101

Alright, we'll keep this to ourselves for now.' Hennessey handed Yellich the passbook. 'Log it into productions with the rest of the stuff and tomorrow phone the building society, find out what you can about Mr Payne, everything and anything, then return to the house of Pinder, and with a team of eager young constables, dig up the garden.'

'Dig . . . not again.'

'The indication is that something, or someone, is buried in the garden.' Hennessey left the coffee beside the vending machine.

'Corpses just keep coming out of the ground.'

'Let's not rush fences, Yellich . . . one stage at a time.'

'Roger that, boss.'

Hennessey returned to the interview room. As he did so, Benson and Pinder leaned away from each other as if they had been huddled in conversation in his absence. He sat down and switched the tape recorder on. 'The time is 1811. I am going to ask the people present in the room to identify themselves.'

'Benson, Stanley, of Benson, Hardwick and Benson, duty solicitor.'

'Jeffrey Pinder.'

'Chief Inspector Hennessey. The place is Micklegate Bar Police Station, City of York division of the North Yorkshire Police. Right, Mr Pinder, a number of items have been recovered from your house, items such as jewellery, watches, photographic equipment . . . which we believe to be the proceeds of burglary. Have you anything to say about them?'

'Things I picked up on the way.' Pinder wasn't giving anything away.

'Tomorrow we are going to dig up your garden,' Hennessey said quietly and once again caused a scowl to creep across Pinder's face. 'We're going to find something there, aren't we?'

Silence.

A shrug of shoulders.

A scowl, a glare, a man who didn't like being proved wrong, did like things going his way and only his way and didn't like it when they didn't.

'Think about it overnight, Mr Pinder. It's the old story: the more you help us, the more you help yourself. You'll now be taken to the charge bar and charged with receiving stolen goods.'

'What proof have you that the items you mention are stolen?'

'The instinct of an elderly and experienced police officer, Mr Benson.'

Pinder shrugged. 'Yeah . . .' he said, 'they're stolen. I was moving them for a team of boys.'

Hennessey smiled. 'That's the right attitude, Mr Pinder. More like that and it will be reflected in your sentence. Who are the boys?'

'Call themselves the Rawcliffe Fleet.'

'The Rawcliffe Fleet, as in fleet of ships?'

'Yes.'

'They won't turn windows on their own turf so they travel across the city to Clementhorpe and turn windows there. Bring the stuff to me. I give them cash then unload it where I can, second-hand shops . . . in the Vale, not York. Too much risk of someone going in and seeing their camera or wedding ring. Second-hand shops will pay cash, no questions asked, sell it on to the public.'

'Any names for the Rawcliffe Fleet?'

'"Dinger" . . . one has that nickname, "Dinger" . . . another is called "Camel".'

'Camel,' Hennessey echoed.

'"Rusher" is another . . . those are the main men in the gang.'

'Alright . . . we'll see what the community constable knows about them, but since you are co-operating . . . what are we going to find in your garden?'

Silence.

George Hennessey drove home. Having worked late, the drive was pleasingly free of rush-hour traffic and he arrived at the outskirts of Easingwold half an hour after leaving Micklegate Bar Police Station, just as dusk was gathering. He drove through the centre of Easingwold and, as always, could not help himself glancing at a certain stretch of pavement in the town which held a terrible significance for him. He drove out of the town on the Thirsk Road and his heart leapt as he noticed a silver BMW parked ahead of him. He slowed down and turned into the driveway of a four-bedroomed detached house, in front of which, half on, half off the kerb the BMW was parked. A dog barked excitedly at the sound of his car on the gravel, and at the same time the front door of the house opened and a brown mongrel shot out and ran and jumped up at Hennessey as he stepped out of the car. A younger man followed the dog and stood smiling at Hennessey.

'Evening, Dad,' the younger man said. 'I let myself in, as you see.'

'Evening, Charles.' Hennessey ruffled the mongrel's ears. 'And hello to you too, Oscar.'

Inside the house, Oscar, now calm, though clearly delighted to have Hennessey home, father and son sat at the table in the kitchen, drinking tea.

'Still not got there?' Charles Hennessey smiled as he read the piece of paper.

'Not yet.' Hennessey followed his son's gaze. 'It's strange the same thirty-two names were barked out each morning for five years with one or two arrivals and one or two departures in that time, but the form remained very cohesive . . . and as I grew older it grew to be a significant group, a significant influence on my life, but I can't recall all the names. I know there were thirty-two because I achieved the distinction of being bottom of the class, once. Thirty-second out of thirty-two.'

Charles Hennessey grinned.

'So, because I never forget that, I know there were thirty-two and I can remember twenty-eight. But they'll come . . . I have faith.'

'Heavens, they'll come, you're like a dog with a bone, or a horse with the bit between its teeth. The determination to see things to completion, it's what makes you a good copper.'

'Well, that's all very well if I and all of us had endless time, but we don't, we are all time limited. Still, there's days enough left yet. The one thing I do regret is not being able to go back and visit my school – it was knocked down to make room for a block of flats. A certain anchor has gone. I really envy folk who can go back and revisit their school. But I'm going back to Greenwich soon.'

'Really?' Charles Hennessey sipped his tea. 'Taking a day's leave?'

'No . . . a case . . . the four skeletons found.'

'That's your case? I did wonder. Saw the evening paper. There's a Greenwich connection?'

'One of the mis pers who we think may be one of the bodies recovered had a home address in Greenwich. Don't recognize the name – no reason why I should. Quite posh now . . . as I recall it, probably even posher now.'

105

'Or less . . . but it's hard to imagine anywhere in London being not sought after, seems that some areas are more sought after than others, but they're all sought after. Can't understand why. I'd hate to have to live there.'

'I couldn't go back, not if I was able to . . . your mother keeps me here.'

'Yes . . .' Charles Hennessey looked around him. 'You seem to be quite comfortable, you and your best friend here, but you should have got married again – it couldn't have been easy bringing me up alone.'

'It wasn't, it was damned hard, but like all difficult experiences, it had its reward. I wouldn't have missed it for the world. I had help remember . . . the string of ladies that came and "did" for me . . . and the force was good. So what are you doing this week?'

'I'm in Leeds, High Court Case . . . a shooting outside a night-club in Bradford. I am for the Crown.'

'Leading?'

'Yes. I have an assistant, a Mr Warren, new man, still cutting his teeth but full of promise. The police have put together a formidable case; there's no defence. The defence barristers are struggling – no points of law to argue, no argument at all; in fact they have already been reduced to trying to discredit the witnesses. How far away were you when you saw the incident? How much had you to drink? They're fighting a losing battle and they know it – it's in their voices . . . the sense of hopelessness comes through.'

'I see. The only thing that can save them now is a perverse jury, which has been known to happen.'

'Has indeed.'

It was George Hennessey's experience, albeit infrequent, to see a flawless prosecution case presented to a jury, that had revealed itself to be 'perverse' in legal jargon by returning a 'not guilty' verdict, and the clearly very guilty felon had been allowed to walk free.

'Early days yet. I think they'll plea bargain. Right now they're both going "NG" to attempted murder. It wouldn't surprise me if tomorrow or Thursday they didn't ask to go "G" to the lesser charge of malicious wounding . . . it's what I would advise them to do if I were their counsel. If they do, we'll accept, it would free up a lot of court time and they'd still get a hefty penalty. Their wretched victim has still got in excess of one hundred and forty shotgun pellets in her body that can't be removed . . . so medical testimony informed us this afternoon. Her skin is turning green about the area of wounding . . . lead poisoning apparently.'

'Not funny.'

'Not funny at all, especially if you are only nineteen and enjoyed disporting yourself in a bikini. Her bikini days are over . . . single blast from a shotgun . . . from about forty feet, but it made a terrible mess.'

'It would do.' Hennessey poured himself another cup of tea. 'Drug-related?'

'Believed to be. The police couldn't discover a motive and the witnesses are clearly being intimidated.'

'Sounds like the tip of a very big iceberg.'

'Sounds it.'

'So, how are the children?'

'Thriving. Looking forward to seeing grandad during the half term next month.'

'Not, I may say, as much as grandad is looking forward to seeing them.'

Later that evening, Charles Hennessey having taken his leave after a warm father and son hug, George Hennessey put a pre-cooked casserole into the oven to heat up and then walked with Oscar to the back of the house, to the lawn, and stood on the lawn and surveyed the garden, as Oscar criss-crossed the lawn.

He and his wife, Jennifer, had bought the house whilst he was still a young constable. When they had bought the house, the rear garden was an unimaginative expanse of grass, too big for a lawn, too small for a football pitch and longer than it was broad. Jennifer had paced out the dimensions of the garden, and scaled them down to produce a plan which she drew one evening, sitting at the breakfast bar and whilst heavily pregnant with Charles. The lawn, she had decreed, would be divided in two, width ways, the division being marked by a privet, in the centre of which would be a wrought-iron gate. The area between the house and the privet would be left as lawn, whilst the area beyond the privet would be an orchard and also the location for garden sheds. The final ten feet of the garden would be the 'going forth', a term she had learned from Francis Bacon's essay 'Of gardens', and would be left in a wild state, although a pond would be dug and native amphibia allowed to colonize it. The plan complete, the youthful George Hennessey was handed a spade and began work, to bring the plan to fruition.

The following summer, Jennifer, then just twenty-three years of age, and proud mother of a three-month-old son, had been walking in Easingwold when, as witnesses described, her legs just seemed to collapse. Folk rushed to her aid, believing her to have fainted, but no pulse could be found. She was pronounced 'condition black' upon arrival at hospital: deceased. The doctors could only ascribe her death to 'sudden death syndrome', which happens, and is occasionally reported but which is not understood, but which seems to affect only the young and healthy who, as in Jennifer Hennessey's case, would be calmly walking along the pavement when life suddenly leaves them and they collapse as if in a faint. George Hennessey had scattered his wife's ashes in the garden, her garden, and then set out to bring up their son, alone, and to build the garden to her design. Each day he would stand in the garden, rain or shine, and 'talk' to his wife whom he 'knew' was there, listening with interest. And one day, one summer's afternoon, he told her of the new love in his life, assuring her that his love for her would not ever diminish, but his new-found lady friend and he had mutual interests which they could each answer, and upon saying that, had felt a rush of warmth which could not be explained by the rays of the setting sun alone.

Later, casserole eaten, an account of the Peninsular War read whilst the meal settled, he then fed Oscar and he and animal, man and dog, took their evening stroll together. Later still, George Hennessey walked into Easingwold, to the Dove Inn, and, as was his habit, enjoyed a pint of stout just before last orders were called.

Five

In which a house is explored and yet another corpse is revealed.

WEDNESDAY, 09.00–11.30 HRS

'Mr Payne,' Yellich repeated. 'James Payne . . . no address, no age, just a name.'

'I'll see what we have, sir.' The voice on the phone was male, efficient, a warm voice, thought Yellich, it would be nice in a lady's ear in the middle of the night. 'Can I call you back, please, save you waiting?'

'Certainly.' Yellich replaced the receiver. He stood and walked from his desk, made a mug of coffee and returned with it to his desk and began to read the papers he had found in his pigeonhole when he had signed in that morning. He glanced at each one, scan-reading them; nothing he felt to be of note – circulars in the main, certainly nothing personally for him, nothing about any active case. He glanced out of the window – the weather promised to hold, being cloudy but dry, though he pondered that a little rain would help his garden no end. His phone rang. He snatched it up.

'Collator, sir.'

'Yes.'

'We have a record of a Mr James Payne as a missing person . . . That's the only record we have. I could check nationally if you wish.'

'I don't think that will be necessary somehow,' Yellich replied. 'Thanks very much. Could you have the file sent up to me, please?' He replaced the receiver and reached for the telephone directory, looked up the number of the Whitby and Scarborough Building Society, York branch, and dialled it.

'Payne? Not a customer I know.' The manager's voice was crisp, businesslike, a little detached, a little cold. In contrast to the collator's voice his was probably, thought Yellich, not the sort of voice that a woman would find comforting in the dark of the night or at any other time. 'If you want any detailed information you will have to let me phone you back so that I can confirm that I am talking to the police.'

'Of course.'

'In fact before we go on I'd like to do that. Who do I ask for – didn't quite catch your name?'

'Yellich. DS Yellich, Micklegate Bar Police Station.' Yellich gave the number.

'Hardly worth a phone call, we are only round the corner from you . . . anyway.' The manager hung up and Yellich once again replaced the receiver and waited for it to ring. It rang again within sixty seconds.

'DS Yellich.'

'Mr Wright, of Whitby and Scarborough. Yes, Mr Payne . . . James Payne. We have a customer of that name . . . nice healthy balance, nothing taken out or put in for five years, I see, but that's not unusual, people just leave their nest egg with us ticking away.'

'Ticking . . . you make it sound like a bomb.' Yellich allowed his 'smile' to be heard down the phone line.

'Mr Payne's account is our highest-yielding account, Mr Yellich, paying nearly ten percent interest per annum and that's on the balance, not the principal sum deposited.'

Mr Wright was clearly in no mood for humour. 'We ask for six months notice of withdrawal from this type of account. The point is that it is hardly dormant, it's quite active and so "ticking" is not an unfair way of describing it.'

Yellich felt like saying he was very sorry, but resisted doing so. He had the impression that Wright was a tyrant, a man too used to receiving apologies from quaking junior staff. It would, Yellich believed, do the man good not to receive an apology on this occasion. There was a knock on the frame of the doorway to his office – a junior constable stood there, file in hand. Yellich beckoned him to enter. The constable did so and placed the missing persons file on James Payne on Yellich's desk. Yellich picked it up and asked what address the building society had for Mr Payne.

'Nether Poppleton,' Wright replied. '154, High Ridge Road, Nether Poppleton.'

'Posh,' Yellich commented.

'Well, I did say he had a nice healthy balance.'

'The account is still open?'

'Yes . . . why, should it be frozen?' A note of alarm crept into Wright's voice and Yellich was relieved to find that Wright was capable of human emotion.

'I should think so. If it is the same Mr Payne, he has been missing for the last five years. And the address you have is the address given here as his home address, so we have to assume it is. A businessman . . .'

'A retailer . . . yes, and as I look back . . . I have his account on the screen . . .'

'We have his passbook . . . not in my hand, I hasten to add.'

'Well, it seems that the account was quite active, deposits and withdrawals aplenty and then nothing about five years ago. Last transaction was a deposit of £150 in the December . . .'

'He was reported missing at that time.' Yellich read the file and suddenly read that Mr Payne was known to the police for fraud and theft. 'Do you vet your clients before letting them open an account?'

'Of course. A letter from a solicitor, a bank providing character references, some form of proof of identify. Why?'

'Nothing . . . how long had Mr Payne had a bank account with you?'

'For . . . for . . . heavens, a long time . . . thirty years. Must have opened it when he was in his early twenties . . . but why do you ask if we vet our clients?'

'Can't tell you. An issue of confidentiality.'

'That's very one-sided of you, Mr Yellich, considering the information I have just given you.'

'Yes it is, Mr Wright, but that's the way of it. This is a police inquiry.' He could feel Wright suppress a temper outburst. 'Well, thanks, Mr Wright, you've been most helpful.' He replaced the phone without waiting for Wright's reply.

His coffee still warm enough to drink, Yellich settled back in his chair and read the missing persons report on one James Payne.

Mr Payne was a bachelor when he had been reported missing five years earlier. He had lived alone in a four-bedroomed detached house in Nether Poppleton and could have been missing for some weeks before he was reported as such: the neighbours became concerned that he hadn't been seen for some days, his car hadn't moved from where it was parked at the side of the road instead of its more usual place in the driveway and the garden had become noticeably overgrown. The police had been called, entry forced, and a neat and tidy house was discovered, no calls on the answerphone, no sign of violence and no James Payne. A spare set of house keys had been found and were attached to the file. The man had indeed disappeared. He had been a businessman and owned a small chain of off-licences in the working-class areas of York, in the estates of Clementhorpe, Acomb, Rawcliffe, Osbaldwick, Tang Hall and Holgate. Yellich pondered the locations, and pondered the inhabitants, whose council-house, terraced-house living, poor employment prospects, actual unemployment, could be escaped from with a few cans of extra-strength lager bought from James Payne's shops, possibly with the proceeds of petty crime. Prolong the pain with Payne, escape the pain with Payne. One or the other. The interested officer: DC Thomas Bull. Yellich remembered him leaving Micklegate Bar, having transferred to a Lancashire force for personal reasons. He'd visited the off-licences owned by Payne. Payne had evidently had a 'hands-off' approach: each 'offie' had a manager and three or four staff who worked a shift system and the last time Payne had been seen had been over a month previous. 'He lets us get on with things,' a manager had been quoted as saying. 'So long as the books balance and we're in the black, then he's a happy bunny.' He had kept work and private life well apart, never socialized with his staff, who in turn knew nothing of his private affairs. Each 'offie' was doing well, 'ticking over, nice and steady, in the black'. No one knew of any enemies or of any reason why he would want to disappear. His neighbours too knew nothing of him; he was spoken of as a man who kept himself to himself.

The police on the other hand knew quite a lot. He had track for theft and crimes of violence, had pulled an eight stretch in Full Sutton for his involvement in a security van hold-up – quarter of a million pounds were appropriated.

He was caught because of a partial thumbprint on a counter top after the robbery had been committed. Four men had been involved but Payne's actual part was not determined and the 'job' had been completed without anyone being injured. He didn't finger anyone else and went down for eight, considered lenient, clearly benefiting from an inexperienced judge and the traditional reluctance of newly appointed judges to impose severe sentences. Payne too had clearly expected a heavier sentence because he was heard to mutter, 'Thank you, Father Christmas,' as he was taken down. The money was never recovered. He had kept his nose clean in Full Sutton and breathed free air after serving five of the eight. He opened his first two 'beer offs' – and here Yellich recalled that Thomas 'Tommy' Bull was from Sheffield, where off-licences are known uniquely as 'beer offs' and the term had crept into Tommy's recording – shortly after leaving prison, clearly using his share of the proceeds of the robbery. After that, Payne had gone straight, apparently; at the very least, he had avoided further prosecution for any other offence. He had lived a quiet life and had not come to the notice of the police, until reported missing.

Yellich looked at the photograph of James Payne as contained in the file. He was tall, probably considered handsome, steely eyed, well dressed, pictured leaning proudly on the bonnet of a Jaguar. The background of the photograph intrigued Yellich: it was England, certainly, unmistakably, but there was a certain softness about the landscape, a flatness, the vegetation seemed a little different, richer, he thought, than that which he was used to. It was England of the southern counties.

Definitely.

Yellich took the photograph from the file, removing it from the solitary paperclip which held it in place – a little lax on 'Tommy' Bull's part, he thought, the photograph ought to have been stapled. On the reverse he saw had been written, 'Devon, with Sue, just me and you'. The date of the photograph as written under the legend was June of the year in which he disappeared. Once again, Yellich felt the poignancy he always felt when looking at photographs which had been taken just before a tragedy had befallen the person or persons pictured. Even if the person concerned was as unpleasant as James Payne had allegedly been unpleasant. He was pleased with his powers of observation and pleased that the knowledge of the country he loved had clearly developed to the extent that he could place a location, albeit roughly. He was right about the location – can't get much more 'southern counties' than Devon, especially since the next county to the south is Cornwall and the Cornish consider themselves a breed apart, so Yellich had observed. Not unlike Yorkshiremen in that respect. He tapped the photograph. But who was Sue? A man who lived alone, kept himself to himself, who was a private person, had nonetheless had a relationship with a lady called 'Sue' that had been sufficiently successful that they had holidayed together in Devon just a few months before he had disappeared. 'Sue', he thought, would be a very useful person to have a chat with. Whoever, wherever she is. If she still 'is'. Yellich glanced at his watch. Still not yet 10 a.m.

George Hennessey stood on the pavement outside Jeffrey Pinder's house. A small crowd had gathered but had kept a respectful distance. The sergeant and constables dug the rear garden, prodding for unconsolidated soil. His presence would not be needed until, and only if, any human remains or some other suspicious material was found. The council houses on the estate seemed small, to his eye, tightly packed together, but hedgerows in front of the gardens provided a means of privacy. Then his mobile purred. He disliked mobiles, disliking them almost as much as motor cars, though for much less personal reasons, but had grudgingly conceded to their advantages. Being able to summon help without having to search for a public phone box being, he thought, their greatest advantage. The price exacted for said advantage, that of being obliged to listen to one-sided conversations in a public place, was heavy (unless, he found, one happened to be listening to one side of an argument). He answered it.

'Hennessey.'

'Yellich here, boss. I've read the mis per file on James Payne, one very interesting character.'

'Really?'

'Yes, really . . . couple of things I'd like to do if I am not needed.'

'Not needed, yet, Yellich, thanks. If we find anything I'll be able to handle it, plenty of uniforms here. Where are you going?'

'Inside.'

Jeffrey Pinder sat across the table from Yellich. He was dressed in denims and blue shirt, lightweight shoes. He looked sullenly at Yellich. 'Didn't expect to see you so soon,' he said.

'Oh?' Yellich took a packet of cigarettes and offered him one. Pinder snatched it. Yellich flicked the disposable lighter and lit the cigarette for him. He put the cigarettes back in his pocket.

'Yeah. Thought you'd let me sweat for a few days.'

'Did you?'

'Yes. You're not going to smoke yourself?'

'Nope. Don't smoke.'

'I see . . . this is just to win me over, is it?' Pinder held up the cigarette.

'Yes.' Yellich nodded. 'You could say that. It's the name of the game. How is it in here?'

'Better than many nicks. It's a new nick. Has comforts that older prisons don't.'

'How well did you know James Payne?'

'Hardly at all.'

'Well, you won't be able to do anything with his passbook, and the hundred thousand therein.'

Pinder shot a glance at Yellich.

'I contacted the building society, they've frozen the account.'

Pinder smiled and shrugged. 'Just one day.'

'Sorry?'

'I was waiting until the fuss about his disappearance died down then I was going to withdraw the money. Try to anyway. I was getting to think it was about safe.'

'We're digging up your garden.'

Pinder's head sagged.

'So there is something buried there?'

Pinder drew on the cigarette and shrugged his shoulders.

'We'll find it, whatever it is.'

'Well, when you do, come back and have another chat. And bring some cigarettes with you.'

'You realize you are in a lot of bother? More than just the stolen goods we found in your house?'

'Well . . . anyway, how did you come to call on me?'

'Told you, someone a long time ago recalls you walking off with his pen, a small black ballpoint. Same type of pen that was found in the mouth of a skeleton which was dug up by some waste ground, next to a place of employment from which you were sacked.'

'Oh, yes . . .'

'And in your house we found clothing, female clothing, odd for a single man living alone.'

'Not so odd really. I've known odder.'

'As I have, but the point is that the clothing bore the name of a girl who disappeared in York twenty years earlier – the nametag was stitched into the collar. We have yet to formally identify the corpse but we believe that it will be one of the four skeletons that we unearthed earlier this week.'

Pinder shrugged.

'Things are bad for you, Jeffrey. Are we going to find Payne's body in your garden?'

A pause.

Pinder looked at Yellich. Yellich knew that the answer to his question was 'yes'.

'Look, Jeffrey, if you think I am kidding about digging up your garden, I assure you I'm not. If you are being stubborn so as to make work for us, then that is OK, we can cope with that. But if you are being silent because you are clinging to the hope that we are bluffing . . . well, you're on to a loser there, because your garden is being dug.' Yellich paused. 'And when we dig, we go down until we are sure we are digging consolidated soil. You go down so far you eventually realize you are digging soil in which nothing has ever been buried. We go down to there.'

Pinder glanced at the cream-painted walls, at the opaque glass window. Yellich read his thoughts. 'It'll be a long time before you breathe free air again . . . maybe never.'

Pinder glanced at him.

'Your age, Jeffrey . . . mid-fifties . . . it's not the time of life to go down for a long stretch.'

'It was self-defence.' He spoke the words quietly.

'Good man,' Yellich prompted.

'He's buried under the back lawn, near the house . . . dug the hole over two nights, covered it with a tarpaulin during the day. It's difficult to dig a hole quietly.'

'Can't say I've tried.' Yellich relaxed as well as any person could relax when sitting on a steel-framed chair.

'Later I realized I should have made no secret of it and told nosy Nora next door that I was building a fish pond. So long as I put him in and covered him up at night when she was fast on and then gone ahead and built the pond, or even said I had changed my mind and filled it in again. But I didn't.'

'So, what happened?'

'I did some work for him . . . on his car at home, he ran a Citroën as well as his BMW. A little 2CV . . . just chugged around York in it. Any distance or going out in the evening with a fancy piece he would use the beamer, but the 2CV was playing up . . . Called me, I went over . . . did a little work, finished the job and went home, came back here. Anyway, he followed me . . . an hour or so later . . . burst in accusing me of stealing from his house.'

'And had you?'

Pinder shrugged his shoulders. 'He had plenty.'

'What did you steal?'

'A few clothes . . . he had some clothes.'

'Women's clothes?'

Pinder nodded. 'I like them.'

Yellich said nothing.

'And a few items like watches, jewellery . . . and some money . . . a wad of notes. Anyway, he came bursting in and demanded I return them but the funny thing . . . the real funny thing, he wasn't bothered about the wedge,

and it was a serious wedge, hundreds of quid . . . he
was panicky about the cheap clothing and the jewellery.
Anyway, things were getting heavy, he was threatening
to kill me if I didn't return the rags and rocks . . . then
he lunged at me . . . Hit him with a torch.'

'A torch?'

'A heavy maglite . . . metal cased. He went down. I
just kept hitting him until he was still.'

'Did you kill him?'

'Yes.'

'I mean did you make sure he was dead?'

'No . . . but later I checked for a pulse, nothing. It was
dark by then . . . went outside and started stripping the
turf off the lawn. First step in digging the hole. He lay
on my living-room carpet for forty-eight hours, before
I dragged him outside and rolled him in. Drove his car
away the first night and left it in York, somewhere . . .
car park behind the railway museum. Wasn't bothered
about my prints being found on it 'cos I had spent the
day working on it. Walked home. Dark night . . . Didn't
want to be seen to be agitated.'

Yellich listened in silence. The man was plausible.
He might even be truthful. If he stuck to his story he
could walk in four years. The self-defence may not be
disprovable – it was, after all, in his home that the incident
took place. He'd be guilty of unlawful disposal of the
dead contrary to Coroner's Rules: that carried a maximum
penalty of four years . . . out in two. Pinder, he thought,
was boxing clever, alright, but Yellich felt there was more
to this man, more to his story. What was unanswered was
why did he lie about not knowing of Mallard's depot, its
remoteness, its proximity to the field in which the bodies
had been found, its proximity to the deserted house at the
edge of the field where, courtesy of a padlock and chain

and grooves carved in the skirting board of an upstairs room, it appeared that the four victims had been restrained and held captive prior to their murder? That was a link which had to be explained.

'I didn't want to admit I had been sacked for thieving,' Pinder said, when Yellich asked him to explain. 'It would look bad.'

'It looks worse now. Now you've been caught out in a lie.'

Pinder remained silent.

'Those bits of jewellery . . . and the clothing . . . in your house, you've half inched them over the years, have you?'

'Yea . . .'

'Remember where from?'

'No . . . not all of them.'

'Remember what you stole from James Payne's house?'

'Yeah . . . I remember because it was so daft . . . he wanted a watch, a woman's watch which had a Mickey Mouse face. I mean, how stupid . . . fancy threatening to kill me for that. A little watch with a picture of Mickey Mouse on the face . . . why would he want that?'

'Probably for the same reason he didn't report you to the police,' Yellich said, standing. 'It probably implicated him in a very serious crime. Glad you're not going anywhere. We'll be talking to you again.' Yellich took two more cigarettes out of the packet and tossed them on to the table.

'Only two? I told you all.'

'For now.' Yellich tapped on the door of the agent's room. 'We'll see how your story checks out.'

Yellich always enjoyed the drive from York out to Full Sutton, the richness of the Vale of York, the expanse of the sky. But he always, always, and that day – that day was no exception – he always enjoyed the drive from Full Sutton back to York much more so.

In York, Yellich drove to Nether Poppleton, to the house once owned by James Payne. Still owned by him, nominally so. No outstanding mortgage to pay, no next of kin to claim his or her inheritance, the house had remained in his name. Now the garden was untidy but not so overgrown as Yellich had expected. Having parked his car, he stood and surveyed the house. It was a detached dwelling, not old, not new build, about thirty years old . . . peeling paintwork, and intact windows. That surprised Yellich, but then this was Nether Poppleton, where the children behave.

'Are you going to buy it?' The voice came from behind Yellich. He turned and perceived the owner to be a late-middle-aged lady, small of frame, piercing eyes behind rimless spectacles, wearing gardening gloves. She had clearly been kneeling behind her privet hedge weeding, or similar, and had stood, curious, at the sound of Yellich's arrival. He had been standing there for a few moments before the woman clearly thought him safe to speak to. 'I wish someone would. It's been empty for so long, you'll get it for a good price.'

'Doubtless I will,' Yellich replied, but didn't give anything of himself away. 'The garden's well kept.'

'The garden's a mess.' The reply was short, snappy, angry.

'I understand it's been empty for a while – the house, I mean?'

'About five years.' Again the retort was angry, almost embittered.

'The garden ought to be more out of control than this after five years. Someone must take care of it.'

'Someone does. Who do you think? It's bang opposite

my house, I see it each morning . . . the garden got so out of control that I couldn't bear to look at it any more and went over there and hacked it back into place. Now I go in once a fortnight. Cut the privet, mow the lawns, the back as well as the front. Others here about thank me for what I do, prevent it being a real eyesore – blot on the landscape isn't the expression – but does anyone lend a hand? Too busy getting on with their own little lives and their perfect families. Me, I never married. Couldn't be bothered with that. So you're interested in buying it, young man, taking some work off me. How about it?'

'Think not,' Yellich smiled. 'I'm here professionally.'

'Estate agent? Are you going to act for the vendor?'

'Police officer. And no, I'm not acting for anybody, except perhaps Her Majesty's Government and the Crown Prosecution Service. I'm going in the house.'

The woman looked disappointed and interested at the same time. No, Yellich said to himself, you can't accompany me, much as you'd like to do so, even love to do so.

'You must see a lot that goes on in the estate?'

The woman rested a pair of secateurs on top of her hedge and wiped her brow. 'Can't miss some of it. I retired to this house about ten years ago after a career in teaching. I have a headship's pension. I don't like travelling, even short distances. It's the garden during the hours of daylight and books by the fireside in the evening. So "yes", is the answer.'

Yellich, sensing 'miss' to be a potentially profitable source of information, crossed the narrow road and stood nearer her, saving them from shouting at each other. 'So you saw Mr Payne move in?'

'Yes.' The woman's voice softened, as if mollified by being asked for information. 'Yes, I did. He had five friends to help him, not a professional removal company, hired a lorry . . . a large van, like a removal van, and had some friends help him. They did an efficient job of it, moving in quite speedily. It was the summer time, can't recall the exact date, but a hot day, in T-shirts and jeans, the furniture was new . . . and they made a lot of noise, shouting to each other, laughing, letting folk know they'd arrived and that they were not too bothered what folk thought about them. New money, a lottery winner, I thought. It had been for sale for a while, a few months – the outgoing owner was a tight-fisted individual, his asking price was too high. The house didn't sell and it was a buyer's market, so he had to come down and that hurt him.' The woman smiled, she saw that Yellich had seen her smile and added, 'Well, I didn't like him, can't expect to like everybody. Anyway, when it was sold I prayed for a quiet, learned type, or even a family who had a taste for old, solid oak furniture and who talked to each other without raising their voices, but no, no such luck for I – my new neighbour revealed himself to be "the solitary neighbour that I shall be troubled with".'

'*Wuthering Heights.*'

'Very good.' She inclined her head, in salutation and respect.

'Well, even police officers have been known to read once in a while.'

'So I see.' Her eyes dilated.

'Mr Payne . . .' Yellich paused, giving to intuition (a good police officer respects his intuition and goes with it. So he had been told . . . that which started life in police canteen culture had, by the time Yellich joined the force, found its way into cadet training schemes: 'Go with your intuition'). 'Tell me about his friends, the ones who helped him move in. They were a gang of six? Mr Payne and five others?'

'Yes . . . what would you like to know?'

'Well, anything you can recall . . . names, ages . . .'

'Ages . . . well he was middle-aged . . . all were the same age, except two of the three women.'

Yellich took out his notebook. 'Six, so three men, three women?'

'Yes . . . Payne, a large-built man, another man of the same age and height but more muscular than Payne, but by then, at that stage in his life, was running to fat . . . spreading a little round here . . .' She tapped her stomach. 'Have him in my garden for a week, I'd have him back in shape in no time. He was quiet, the quietest of the lot. Payne did all the shouting and laughing, he had an east London accent.'

'Did he?'

'Yes, he did, very "cor blimey", very "diabolical liberty", very "on the manor guvnor", "laughed, I nearly cried, know what I mean" – that sort of person.'

Yellich wrote in his notepad. It was a pertinent point.

'You'd notice that,' the woman said. 'Not of this county. He wasn't anyway.'

'Thanks . . . and you are?'

'Carter, Phyllis, Miss.'

'Miss Carter,' Yellich parroted.

'The third man was very small, very slightly built, he too was getting a little wide about his waist, and a little thin on top. He scurried about like a little squirrel, carrying anything light enough for him to carry, so if Mr Payne and the other well-built man carried a chest of drawers into the house, the little fella would trot behind them carrying the drawers.'

'I get the picture.'

'Good. Well, a fourth "man" proved to be a woman of that age group, fifties, early rather than late fifties, but very masculine, short but stocky, dressed in overalls . . . short hair . . . At first glance, I thought she was a man, two big ones, two short ones, but then I realized she was a she.'

'I see.'

'Then the other two women were very feminine, arriving in a sports car, walking into the house, not even attempting to help with the furniture moving, just swanned in as though they were going to decide on the decoration and wouldn't pick anything up in case they split their nails . . . summer dresses and high heels . . . sneered at the first woman, who glared at them when they weren't looking at her.'

'Any names you recall?'

'Well . . . one of the glamour pieces was called "Babs", I presume short for Barbara.'

'Interesting.'

'Is it?'

'Potentially . . . yes.'

'I saw her again a couple of times and came to understand that she was Mr Payne's girlfriend . . . The other girl – didn't get to know her name and only saw her that once. The other large man was 'Izzy' by name – I presume it was a nickname, but which unlike "Babs" could be derived pretty well from anything. No names for any of the other's. The glamour pieces were younger, in their early thirties, I would say. So he settled in, a brash, jovial, slightly overweight, large-built man. Found out he owned off-licences. Oh my, so much for my erudite neighbours! Lived alone except when "Babs" visited, which she did, for days at a time, but never moved in. He was quiet in terms of his habits, no sound from the house, no loud music, no arguments, kept on top of the garden for the rest of that summer. Then, around late November, possibly

December, I noticed the garden getting overgrown, a little, being winter, but excess growth of the vegetation became noticeable, as did things like litter beginning to accumulate on the lawn . . . his big car not moving . . . and left parked on the road. The road, as you see, is narrow and we co-operate with each other by putting our cars in our driveways whenever possible . . . leaving them out on the road for a short while only and Mr Payne followed suit. The curtains didn't move, the other little car he had was not seen at all, the lights went off and on at the same time each day. Eventually his car was towed away.'

'Timer devices.'

'That's what we thought. No panic at all at first – off with "Babs" to Crete or somewhere for a little winter sun, no reason to tell us where he was going, we don't live in and out of each other's houses here, but after three weeks we began to become . . . well, curious. We must have let a full month go by before we called the police. They forced entry without doing a great deal of damage. Nothing in the house to cause concern, so there was nothing they could do. They found a set of door keys and secured the property. The officer said he was really pushing it to accept it as a missing person report, but he would do just to be safe because Mr Payne was a bachelor with no known family, so no one to report him missing. But we seem to have been exonerated . . . five years now, no Mr Payne, no worried girlfriend.'

'No worried girlfriend,' Yellich repeated as a chill went through him, despite the warm, dry September day.

Having thanked Miss Carter for her information, Yellich re-crossed the narrow suburban street to the house once owned, and still technically owned, by one James Payne. He took the set of keys from his pocket and walked up to the front door and unlocked it. The air inside the house was stale, almost unhealthily so, and so Yellich remained by the front door for a few moments, allowing the old, stale air to mix and mingle with the fresh air. He spent the time sifting through the mail which had accumulated inside the front door. He was, after all, by all accounts, the first person to cross the threshold since the police had forced the door five years earlier. It was all so-called 'junk' mail, nothing at all of a private or personal nature. He removed it by the armful to his car and placed it in the boot, with the intention of disposing of it at a council waste site. Leaving it where it was, he thought, constituted a fire hazard. Having removed all the mail, Yellich returned to the house and, the air within now more breathable, he walked into the hall, into the kitchen and opened one of the windows in the kitchen, thus causing a through flow of air which would further allow the house to ventilate.

He walked from room to room, taking the opportunity to open windows wherever he could upstairs and down-stairs. He did not know what he was looking for. He decided that the first thing to do was to 'read' the house. It was after all still, allegedly, in the state that it had been when James Payne had driven away in the small blue Citroën to confront Jeffrey Pinder about the theft of a watch with a Mickey Mouse design on the face. Payne presumably intended to return that same day.

The first thing that struck Yellich was how neat the house was – it had the hard feel to the décor that single men's houses have (a house with a woman's touch will be softer somehow in respect of its decoration, such was Yellich's repeated observation), but single men's homes are also very untidy. This was a clear exception. Not even a single unwashed plate in the kitchen sink. After five years, dust had accumulated on the washed plates, and cutlery on the draining board beside the sink had grown a film of mould and cobwebs, but had been clearly washed, awaiting only putting away. In the living room, which ran the width of the house, all was neat and tidy; the books were on the shelves, such few books as there were, mostly book club offers, the many video cassettes also neatly stacked. Payne was clearly a man who had liked order in his life, a man who was on top of things, a man who liked to be in control. Yellich went upstairs – the stairway he found to be quite narrow as with most houses of that era. Upstairs was a bathroom, again neatly kept with an array of cleaning materials, although by then, like the remainder of the house, covered in dust and cobwebs. The large bedroom contained a double bed, made up, and a built-in wardrobe. Yellich opened the wardrobe. Clothing still hung neatly, or was laid neatly in drawers within the wardrobe. He inspected the remaining two bedrooms. One contained a single bed, not made up, empty wardrobe and drawers, the other contained a bunk bed, also unmade and similar empty furniture. A family home without the family to make it come alive. It was a harsh house, even when inhabited it must, thought Yellich, have been a house with neither life nor soul. He was instantly grateful for the warmth he experienced each time he set foot over the threshold of his house. He returned downstairs and sat in the armchair that faced the front window, through which he could see his car, and behind the car, on the other side of the road, the hedge of Miss Carter's property. Yellich could imagine the disappointment of the woman when she realized the nature of the new owners of this house: the mix would be that of oil and water.

He returned his attention to the issue at hand. The occupant of this house had left the house to attempt to recover property stolen from him by Jeffrey Pinder. He was, by Pinder's account, clearly very anxious to recover possession of it. Very anxious. There had been no evidence of any item foreign to the house. The clothing in the wardrobe was male. If Pinder had stolen items of female clothing, it hadn't been from this house. But he had stolen a watch. So where would he have stolen a watch from? Only two places in the house were left to be explored, the attic and the garage. Pinder would not have gotten into the attic. Sneaking into the bedroom of his customers' houses on the pretext of using the bathroom was one thing, but he couldn't have got into the attic of this, or any house, not without coming to the attention of the householder. That left only the garage . . . and where, Yellich mused, where could a jobbing car mechanic go without attracting suspicion but the garage? Yellich stood, he walked out of the house, leaving by the front door, which he allowed to remain open, and down the driveway to the garage. The garage was of a usual suburban variety, sheets of corrugated asbestos forming the walls and on the roof, and wooden doors, painted cream to match the house. The doors had windows set in them, through which Yellich, with the advantage of a police officer's height, could clearly see. He saw that the interior of the garage was empty. It was empty in that it was devoid of a motor vehicle, or of anything suspicious, but it did contain what appeared to be a workbench at the far end. He turned and strolled back up the drive, across the road and stood in front of Miss Carter's hedge. He heard her digging with a trowel. 'Excuse me,' he said. Miss Carter stood up, promptly. 'Yes?'

'When the police forced entry to the house on that occasion . . . ?'

'Yes?' She wiped her brow.

'Do you remember if they searched the garage as well as the house?'

Phyllis Carter paused. 'I don't think they did . . . no . . . I don't think so . . . what happened . . . what happened about the garage . . . they were very thorough . . . they went into the attic.'

'You went into the house with them?'

'No, they wouldn't allow us to, but they told us they had checked the house thoroughly, including the attic . . . but what did they do about the garage? What did they do? Ah, yes, I remember, they looked into it, there are windows in the door and windows at the back of the garage, they looked in both . . . so they saw the whole of the interior of the garage, and being able to see that it didn't contain the body of the missing Mr Payne, they didn't force entry. Nor reason why they should.'

'No reason at all.' Yellich smiled. 'Well, thank you again, Miss Carter.'

Yellich returned to the house. He went into the kitchen and opened cupboard doors looking for keys hanging from hooks, bunches that might contain the garage key. Wherever Payne had kept his keys, he had not kept them on hooks behind cupboard doors. But beneath a cupboard, in a small space of about one foot high, he found a plastic tub that had once contained margarine. In the tub were assorted items, slender batteries of the type Yellich used in his bedside alarm clock, a screwdriver, a pair of scissors, a padlock and keys for same, and a large key that fitted a mortise lock, and which was labelled 'garage'.

The lock in the garage door was dry, it hadn't turned in five years, and gave only grudgingly to the key when it was turned forcefully by Yellich. The air in the garage proved to be as stale as the air in the house and so Yellich opened the door widely and paused before entering, taking time to glance up at a blue sky with a few wisps of cloud and watched the twin streaks of a vapour trail of a jet airliner flying from Continental Europe across England towards Ireland and the Atlantic and, eventually, to North America. He imagined the pilot telling his passengers that they were flying over the north of England, that those passengers on the port side of the aircraft may be able to see the medieval city of York below. Yellich then considered matters closer to hand and entered the garage. He walked across the concrete floor of the garage to the workbench, which he saw had a series of drawers beneath the working surface. He opened the right-hand drawer. His heart leaped. In the drawer was a collection of jewellery and watches of the type favoured by females, a large collection, and in the middle of the three drawers was clothing, female clothing but only underclothing and a T-shirt. He picked out one or two items, and examined each for names, just as Melita Campion had stuck a name tag into the blouse she had been wearing on the day she had disappeared. One item of clothing had such a name tag; it was clear to Yellich from where Jeffrey Pinder had collected Melita's blouse and items of female underclothing, and from where he had obtained the watch that James Payne was so anxious to retrieve. The drawers were trophy drawers, the trophies had come from murdered young women. And it had been a massive, massive, oversight on Payne's part to leave them. He replaced the item of clothing, a pair of briefs, and slid the drawer shut. He left the garage and locked it behind him. He secured the house and drove, anxiously, across the city to Clementhorpe, to where he expected that, by then, DCI Hennessey and his team had discovered the remains of James Payne.

'You found it quite quickly.' Louise D'Acre stood at the edge of the shallow grave looking down at the skeleton. 'I mean, no other part of the gardens seems to have been . . . shall I say, explored.'

'Stroke of luck really,' Hennessey replied. 'We were delayed in setting out this morning . . . came here expecting to have to excavate the garden until we found something of interest, just arrived here when I got a call from DS Yellich on my mobile . . . he'd just been to see the occupant of this house, ex-occupant I should say . . . well, maybe he can keep the tenancy . . . anyway, he told Yellich where we could find the body. So we dug where indicated.'

'And here we are.'

'And here we are, as you say. Not deep. Didn't take us long.'

'Do you know who he is, or was?'

'Believed to be one James Payne, aged about forty-five when he died.'

Louise D'Acre nodded. 'It's male, middle years . . . large build . . . clothed when he was buried, see the remnants of what appears to have been a suit, and the shoes are clearly visible, as you can see. Have you been told the cause of death?'

'The informant says fractured skull, occasioned in self-defence.'

'He would, wouldn't he?' Louise D'Acre smiled. 'And unless you can find witnesses or evidence to the contrary, the law is obliged to give him the benefit of the doubt. As is right and proper, of course.'

'Indeed . . . ah . . .' Hennessey turned, his eye caught by a sudden movement, 'DS Yellich.'

'Good morning, Mr Yellich.' Dr D'Acre smiled for a second time.

Hennessey nodded silently in response to Yellich. 'Get anything at the house?'

'I think so, boss. I see you found him. Pinder was telling the truth . . . Mind you, I don't think he could have done anything else once he knew we were going to dig up the garden. All he can do now is work for himself.'

'Or conceal what he knows he can conceal,' Hennessey growled. 'I don't want to appear cynical, but Dr D'Acre here made the point just before you arrived that the Crown will have to give him the benefit of the doubt in respect of his self-defence plea.'

'Well.' Louise D'Acre walked round the grave to view the rear of the skull. She crouched down. Her green coverall seemed to rustle and creak as she did so. 'Difficult to tell from this distance and in this light, but it doesn't appear that he was hit from behind . . . tends to confirm the self-defence theory. A massive fracture to the posterior aspect of the skull would cause him to have to work hard to convince a jury of his self-defence argument.' She stood, but continued to look at the body. 'No gag or restraints that I can see, a shallow, hastily dug grave . . . in his back garden . . . that's not premeditation, that's panic . . . but this is more your department than mine. Well, have you taken all the pictures you want to take?'

Hennessey glanced at the Scenes of Crime Officer, who nodded, and said, 'Yes, sir, every angle, colour and black and white.'

'Well, I needn't hold things up any,' Dr D'Acre said. 'I'll take a few soil samples, but with a corpse of this age, there is no point in taking rectal temperatures . . . he'll be as cold as the clay that has surrounded him these years past. I can do the PM this p.m.' She smiled at her own joke. 'Clumsy that,' she added. 'I can do the post-mortem this afternoon would be a better way of saying it. Did the culprit say what was the weapon he used to defend himself?'

'A maglite. A metal torch,' Yellich said. 'We use them. If you hold them by the lens end they make a formidable weapon, a very hefty cosh indeed. Give anyone a nasty headache.'

'To say the least,' Dr D'Acre said. 'And in this case, more than a nasty headache.' She looked at Hennessey, who began to smile, but stopped as Louise D'Acre froze him with a stare. 'Shall we remove him?'

'Of course.' Hennessey turned. 'Sergeant!'

'Sir!'

'Stretcher and concealment bag.'

'Sir!'

'So –' Louise D'Acre brushed soil from her hands – 'shall we say two p.m. for the post-mortem?'

'Two p.m., agreed,' Hennessey replied warmly although this time avoiding eye contact. 'I'll attend for the police.'

Six

In which the Chief Inspector and his good ser-
geant partake of luncheon.

WEDNESDAY, 13.00–22.00 HRS

H ennessey and Yellich left the scene of the excavation in the small rear garden in the house at Clementhorpe and returned, in separate cars, to Micklegate Bar Police Station. It was, they both felt, an annoyingly short journey and served really only to take their cars to a place where they could be parked in safety. In the car park at the rear of the police station, Hennessey turned to Yellich and smiled. 'Lunch?' he asked.

'Sir? Oh, I was going to get a bite at the canteen, boss.'

'Join me . . . my treat.'

'Well, yes . . . thank you, sir.'

They walked in silence across narrow Micklegate Bar, beneath the medieval stone gateway where once, in ancient times, the head of Harry Hotspur had been impaled as a warning to any who dared defy the Crown, and they then took the steps up on to the wall and walked it, in silence, weaving between the tourists and citizens who walked in the opposite direction. They left the walls at Lendal Bridge, took the bridge, where the 'girls' had once stood soliciting for custom until they were lured into the more lucrative, and safer, massage parlours. From Museum Street, they turned into Lendal, walked past the imposing and graceful Judge's Residence, left into St Helen's Square where two young women played Mozart on clarinet and violin to the approval of a modest crowd, and into Stonegate. On bustling, one-car-wide, pedestrianized Stonegate, Hennessey turned into a snickelway, which Yellich had not known existed. The narrow, covered passage, one of many in the medieval quarter, led to a pub, the Starre Inne, the oldest such establishment in York. They found a corner seat under low beams, beneath a print of a map of 'Yorkshyre', dated 1610 and with 'the famous and fayre citie York, defcribed'.

'Where now?' Hennessey asked after swallowing a mouthful of coarse and meaty Cumberland sausage.

'Sir?' Yellich glanced up from his plate of chilli. The meal was not so expensive, much better than police canteen food, and he saw then why Hennessey preferred to lunch outwith the station.

'The investigation. Where now?'

'Oh . . .' Yellich struggled with a mouthful of food.

'I mean, I think I know where we go, but I'd like your opinion.'

'Well, sir . . . the thing that intrigued me was why James Payne should be so concerned to get the watch back from the pathetic Jeffrey Pinder . . . and a glance in the drawers in the garage of his home, and lo . . . lo and behold.'

'What did you find?'

Yellich told him, enjoying Hennessey's jaw sag as he recounted the items of female clothing found in the drawer of the garage workbench. 'And,' he added, 'with Melita Campion's nametag on a pair of briefs.'

'You've secured the garage?'

'Of course, boss.'

'Well, well, well . . . I don't know where to go after all . . . or maybe I do.'

'Where were you going?'

'To the parents of the girls, if they are still alive, or to any sibling . . . asking for information about the lifestyle, any friends, anything at all. It's certain the girls will be identified. I should think photographs could be superimposed on the photographs of the skulls, that will be the best way to do it. Failing that, dental records . . . but I confess, what you have told me astounds me. You kept it quiet?'

'No, I didn't, this is the first opportunity.' Yellich smiled. 'Came straight from Payne's musty house to Clementhorpe, discovered you had found Payne's remains in Pinder's back garden, we returned to the station, you offered to buy me lunch, and here we are. First opportunity.'

'So, Payne was involved in Melita Campion's murder?'

'Seems so . . . the female clothing in his garage is sufficient to clothe four young women. He was a trophy man.'

'Good heavens, it's closing in faster than I thought.'

'We hope; still a long way to go yet, though.'

'Any more? Anything else to tell me?'

'Actually, yes.'

'Enjoying this, aren't you?' said with a smile.

'Actually, yes.' Yellich returned the smile.

'Go on . . . confess this is proving to be a most profitable lunch.'

'Well, if you had lunched alone you would have returned to find it all written up and laid upon your desk, sir. You're getting it verbally about half an hour before you would have read it.'

'Alright . . . so what else?'

'Well.' Yellich, controlling the moment, forked chilli into his mouth, chewed, swallowed, and continued. 'Correct me if I am wrong here, but when the drunk tottered into the police station and gave information which started the ball rolling, did he not describe four people to be involved in the murder he witnessed?'

'Well, you took the statement, but yes, I think he did.'

'Two tall men, one short man, one woman he first thought to be a man because of her stocky build?'

'Yes . . . without checking the statement, I think that's correct.'

'Well, I had a chat with the lady, and I emphasize lady, who lives across the street from Payne's house, a lady by the name of Carter, very headmistressy, but a keen observer. Anyway, she recalls Payne's friends helping him move in . . . one tall guy, muscular, one very short guy, one very short, stockily built female.'

'The same gang.'

'That's what I thought.'

'Still together, fifteen, twenty years after the first murder. By then they had been joined by two other women, girlfriends of Payne and the other tall man.'

'Names?'

'The tall guy was called by the nickname "Izzy". The girl who was Payne's girlfriend was addressed as "Babs".'

'Barbara.'

'Pretty well certain to be, boss. But, as Miss Carter pointed out, "Izzy" could be derived from anything.'

'"Isambard" springs to mind, but I doubt that will be his name,' Hennessey mused aloud.

Yellich looked pleased with himself. Hennessey, reading his face, reading the look in his eyes, said, 'There's still more to tell me, isn't there?'

'Payne went down for a bullion robbery, got eight years, never grassed on his accomplices, out in five . . . money was never recovered.'

Hennessey leaned back and his shoulder hit the back of the bench upon which he sat, with a thud. 'You have had a fruitful morning.'

'Confess, I rather enjoyed it myself,' Yellich replied.

'So Payne is convicted of one serious crime, linked to an earlier, even more serious crime or crimes, of some years previous. Was apparently still friends with the same people who were party to the murders with him when he disappeared five years ago.'

'Yes.'

'And if the other three were part of the murders, then they were probably part of the bullion robbery.'

'That is my thinking too, skipper.'

'We've got to trace those three people, Yellich.' Hennessey placed his knife and fork side by side on the plate. 'I am attending the PM on Payne now . . . can you address it? Press release, I think.'

'Leave it with me, boss. Thanks for lunch.'

'It was my pleasure –' Hennessey smiled – 'it was my pleasure.'

Hennessey and Yellich stood and left the Starre Inne. It was, Hennessey thought, an excellent lunch, excellent on many levels.

Yellich and Hennessey parted company on narrow Stonegate, small shops and bustling crowds, Hennessey turning left, Yellich turning right. Hennessey walked to York District Hospital, turning left underneath the magnificent York Minster, allowing his lunch to settle as he walked. Yellich, younger, more energetic, walked with a little more urgency back to Micklegate Bar Police Station. He had a press release to prepare. It also occurred to him that he should ask the collator to search for any locally known felon called 'Izzy'. He had enjoyed giving information to DCI Hennessey. He felt to be on a roll, he wanted to keep up the momentum.

Hennessey arrived at York District Hospital at 1.45 p.m., and as he walked across the car park to the slab-sided, medium-rise building he looked for, and saw, the red and white Riley, belovedly owned by Louise D'Acre. It had been, he was once told, her father's first and only car, now it belonged to her, and it was lovingly serviced by a garage, the proprietor of which had made her promise to give him first refusal should she ever wish to sell the vehicle. It was a promise freely given in the knowledge that it would never be sold. If the vehicle, allegedly over fifty years of age and belonging to the previous century, could be kept roadworthy, then Louise D'Acre would bequeath it, in the fullness of time, to one of her children, most likely her son.

Hennessey entered the hospital building and walked to the pathology laboratory, where he changed into green coveralls, and put a disposable paper hat over his head and walked into the dissecting room. Louise D'Acre glanced at him as he entered.

'Just about ready to start,' she said, efficiently.

Eric Filey smiled a warm welcome, in response to which Hennessey nodded, equally warmly.

The skeleton of the man who in life had been James Payne lay on the stainless-steel table at the end of the row of similar tables.

Louise D'Acre peered closely at the skull and examined it with latex-gloved hands. 'Well, there are a number of depressed fractures to the front of the skull.'

'The front?'

'Yes . . . is this significant?'

142

'For the fella's defence team, probably, as we said earlier.'

'You have the murderer, I think?'

'The tenant of the house . . . I mean where the body was found, in the back garden . . .' Hennessey stumbled for words, it was not like him. 'Well, he was the tenant of that council property.'

'I see. Sufficient link for you to be suspicious?'

'Oh, he coughed, like I said, told us where to look for the body. He's arguing self-defence and the blows at the front of the skull would seem to bear that out.'

'There are multiple blows.'

'Really?'

'Yes, really . . . also on the top and rear aspect of the skull, but mainly to the front. If I have to give evidence it would be in support of the self-defence plea. Is the accused a small man?'

'Quite small . . . about five and a half feet tall.'

'Smaller than our friend here.' Louise D'Acre reached for a retractable tape measure and, with the help of Eric Filey, who sprang forward to assist when he saw the tape measure being produced, measured the length of the skeleton. 'Five . . . no . . . six feet in life, possibly six feet one inch, allowing for the soles of the feet and the cartilage which will have disappeared and shrunk respectively . . . and in footwear, perhaps six feet two inches . . . and the angle of the blows . . . the forward most ones are at about forty-five degrees on the top of the forehead. If they were the first blows struck, that would be consistent with the weapon being held by a shorter person, and as he went down, the shorter person continued to rain blows and so we see a progression of depressed fractures going from the front to the back of the skull. Not one in itself would be fatal, I wouldn't have thought, but the accumulation of them all . . . there's six that I can identify, which would probably mean many more blows were struck. If he was striking this man in self-defence, then it was panic driven.'

'Attacked in his home,' Hennessey offered, 'came demanding the return of an item that somewhat light-fingered attacker had purloined earlier that day, some years ago.'

'I see. There appear to be no other injuries . . . nothing that could cause death. Are you certain of his identity?'

'As certain as we can be but we'd like to make sure, of course.'

'I'll remove his jaw, dental records will confirm that. He has had dental care and if he was killed less than eleven years ago, his records will still be on file. I'll extract a tooth and cut it in cross section, that'll give his age plus or minus twelve months. Do you know how old he was when he died?'

'Yes . . . he's a felon . . . well acquainted with the inside of Full Sutton.'

'Really? So identification shouldn't be a problem?'

'Shouldn't be,' Hennessey said, but as he said that he paused, faltered, and then said, 'Dr D'Acre . . . this may be the intuition of an experienced police officer, or it may be the suspicious mind of a man who's been a police officer far too long, but can I request that you photograph the skull before you remove the jaw and any of the teeth?'

'Yes –' Louise D'Acre nodded in understanding – 'yes, of course . . . we'll do it now. Mr Filey, your camera please.'

'Six feet tall, you say?' Hennessey asked.

'Minimum, I'd say.' Louise D'Acre stood back whilst

Eric Filey positioned the camera. 'Could be six one, or two.'

'Broad build, would you say?'

Louise D'Acre glanced at the skeleton, blinked as the camera flashed and then said, 'No, frankly I would say he would be on the slender side. In life he would be considered to be "lanky".'

'If you'd excuse me, please,' Hennessey said, 'just for a minute, I would like to make a phone call. Do you mind if I use the phone in your office?'

'Please . . .' Louise D'Acre smiled, 'help yourself.'

Yellich took Hennessey's call, listened and then said, 'Hold on boss, I've got his file with me' . . . making a long arm . . . 'Yes, got it now' . . . opens it . . . frontispiece . . . scans said front sheet . . . 'five eleven in his stocking feet.'

'Oh . . .' Hennessey groaned as he scanned Louise D'Acre's office wall, her three children, their horse, all lovingly photographed, framed with care, and proudly hung on the wall. 'I had an intuition.'

'Which you must always go with, as you have so often said.'

'Don't know, just couldn't explain it. I suppose that's the nature of intuition, or perhaps it was suspicion. You see I couldn't understand why, if someone, i.e. Pinder, had murdered someone, and had all the time in the world to dispose of the body, and a very large van to carry the body away to some remote place, possibly in little pieces, why he should bury it in his back garden where it was likely to be discovered?'

'Why indeed?' Yellich too was puzzled.

'So I asked Dr D'Acre if she could tell me how tall the corpse was in life. She said, six feet minimum and lanky build.'

'Whereas James Payne in life was five eleven and broadly built.' Yellich paused. 'So who is the person we took from the ground this morning?'

'Exactly!' Hennessey echoed. 'Who is he?'

'I'd better have a chat with Jeffrey Pinder.'

'Think you had.'

'But you know, skipper, it doesn't make sense. I mean, why would Pinder want to link Payne to the murdered girls . . . which he did, remember? Pinder half-inched some female clothing from Payne's trophy drawer, one item of which had Melita Campion's name on it. I mean, why link Payne to those murders and then claim Payne is the corpse that is buried under his back lawn?'

'Puzzling, indeed . . .' Hennessey scanned the smiling faces of the D'Acres: Louise, her daughters, Dianne and Fiona, her son, Daniel, their horse, the beloved Samson. 'I can't think of a clear reason – it only serves to link Pinder to those murders and he wouldn't want that. But it means he is involved in something far more serious than unlawful disposal of the dead following accidental killing in self-defence.'

'I'll drive out to Full Sutton, have a chat with him.'

'If you would. Did you get the press release out?'

'Yes, boss, it'll make the mid-afternoon bulletin on the television and the hourly bulletins on the radio.' Yellich glanced at his watch. 'In fact, the first radio bulletin will have been broadcast, too early to expect a response yet.'

'Of course.'

'Also checked to see if anyone known as "Izzy" is on our records: computer check came back negative.'

'OK. That was worth a try. What were you going to do this afternoon?'

'Read the file on the bullion robbery. Familiarize myself with that. You still at York City?'

'Yes, surprised you can't smell the formaldehyde down the phone, confess it's quite intense. Alright, I think Pinder first – he must be feeling quite smug believing he's looking at a four stretch, max, walk in two, go and unnerve him. See where you get. I have to return to the post-mortem. Dr D'Acre will be waiting for me . . . police presence required.'

'Twice in one day.' Pinder looked relaxed.

'Just tidying up loose ends.' Yellich too adopted a relaxed attitude.

'Got a nail?'

Yellich nodded and handed Pinder a packet of Benson and Hedges. Pinder took one and pocketed the packet. Yellich smiled and gestured for the return of the packet. Pinder shrugged and sent the packet skidding back across the table. Yellich took his lighter, flicked it and offered the flame to Pinder. Pinder sat forward to light his cigarette and as Pinder was drawing the first smoke in, Yellich asked, 'So who is the guy we dug from your garden this morning, because it's not James Payne?'

Pinder spluttered.

Yellich smiled.

Pinder paled and seemed suddenly uninterested in his cigarette.

A pause.

A very long pause.

Pinder's face sagged. 'It was like watching his face fall off,' Yellich would say in days to come.

Yellich knew the silence was set to continue for a very long time, so he broke it. 'You see, Jeffrey, things have moved up a notch for you – you're in a different league now. It is no longer unlawful disposal of the dead . . . it's . . . well, what can it be? Largely depends on how the man was murdered, why he was murdered. Where the real James Payne is, and why . . . why . . . why . . . did you leave the body, as if hidden, but knowing it would be found? You even told us where to look.'

Pinder looked at the ceiling, at the floor, at the opaque pane of glass set high in the wall of the agent's room. He remained silent, but recovered sufficiently to draw on the nail.

'Not playing, eh?' Yellich leaned forward. 'Taking your bat and ball home are you? So where is James Payne?'

Silence.

'And Babs, his glamour piece?'

Silence.

'And Izzy and his glamour piece?'

Silence.

'And where is the small, weasely guy and the short stocky woman that make up that team?'

Silence.

'And what is your connection with the team?'

Silence.

'And what do you know of Melita Campion?'

'Nothing.' Pinder drew deeply on the nail.

Yellich smiled inwardly. Progress, he thought. A response, any response, meant progress. 'Sure?'

'Yes. Sure.'

'Why link Payne to her then?'

'Did I?'

'Well, yes, by implication . . . you told us this morning that when Payne came to your house he didn't want the money you had stolen from him . . .' Yellich turned back the pages of his notebook. 'He was anxious to recover the item of jewellery and female clothing. But not the money which you described as, and I quote, "a serious wedge" and "hundreds of quid".'

148

Pinder shrugged.

'Has Payne got something over you?'

Pinder glanced at Yellich, a split second of eye contact that said, 'Yes, yes he has.'

'OK.' Yellich relaxed and sat back in the chair. 'OK, OK, OK . . . Now you've been in trouble with the police enough times to know the rule . . .'

'Help you and you'll help me?'

'Yes, you can make it hard for yourself or you can make it easy for yourself . . . is another way of putting it.'

Pinder drew a deep breath.

'It can't be your taste for women's clothing. You're not embarrassed about that, and it's harmless. If you like wearing skirts and you keep it to yourself in your house, there's no harm done at all. It isn't even a crime. So, what is it?'

Another sullen silence.

'Can you cope with life in the slammer?'

Pinder shot a glance at Yellich.

'Well, if you wanted us to believe that the corpse in your back garden was Payne, and now we know it isn't, that can only mean seriously foul play. Why would you want us to believe we had found the body of Payne?'

Pinder raised an eyebrow.

'If we had believed the body to be that of Payne, what would the implication of that be?' Yellich asked, thinking aloud. 'Looking at it from Payne's point of view, the answer is that we would stop searching for him in connection with the disappearance of those young women twenty-plus years ago. So we were meant to find their clothing and assorted knick-knacks . . . and we were meant to assume Payne is dead, can't find Izzy and the other two . . . limited police resources, case gathers dust and they get away with it. Was that the plan?'

'Maybe.'

'And where do you figure in all this? And what is the significance of the building society passbook in Payne's name, with one hundred thousand pounds in it and which was found in your possession? The money still untouched . . . was that all part of the plan to fake Payne's disappearance?'

Pinder shrugged his shoulders.

'So, what sort of money must someone have at their disposal if they can afford to give up a hundred thousand?'

Silence.

'The sort of money that comes from a bullion robbery. Has to be.'

Yet another silence. 'Alright, so you were not involved in the murder of the four young women . . . you didn't know Payne's team then, but you got in tow with them later. You had some part to play in the bullion robbery . . . some great or less great part . . . and Payne has something to hold over you that makes it worth your while to help him fake his own death. But whatever it is, you have to think whether it's worth life. And you aren't any spring chicken, Jeffrey – in your case life could very well mean life. Do some thinking tonight. We'll be back to see you.'

Yellich returned to Micklegate Bar Police Station. He found the collator had left a note in his pigeonhole advising him that the file on the bullion robbery had been 'lifted' from the void and was at his disposal. He walked down the narrow corridor in the nineteenth-century building to his office, switched the electric kettle on and walked to his desk and picked up the phone. He pressed a four-figure internal number.

'Collator!'

'DS Yellich,' he said. 'I'm in the building now. Can you send the file up, the file on the bullion robbery? Thanks.' He replaced the phone and made a cup of instant coffee, allowing it to cool as he glanced out of his office window, waiting for the requested file to arrive. The weather was beginning to cloud over, but tourists were thick on the walls, all good for the city's coffers. There was a tap on the doorframe of his office. He turned. A cadet stood in the doorway; his manner seemed to Yellich to be a mixture of eagerness and nervousness.

'That the file I asked for?' Yellich smiled.

'Yes, sir . . . the collator asked me to bring it to you, sir.'

'Thank you. If you could put it on my desk . . . thanks.' Yellich returned his gaze to the window and when he heard the cadet's footfall fade in the corridor, he walked to his desk, sat down and picked up the file and, cradling the mug of coffee in one hand, began to read.

The bullion robbery had taken place in York eight years previously and £800,000 had been stolen. It spoke of 'an inside job'. It was neat, clean, well executed. What had happened, Yellich read, and well recalled the incident as he did so, though he wasn't one of the interested officers, was that the vehicle containing the money had been forced to stop on a quiet country road just outside the city, the occupant forced out of the vehicle and the money, in notes, removed in four large sportsbags transferred from one vehicle to the other. The money had been on its way from England to Switzerland via Hull, a ferry, and car journey to Zurich. Not a great deal of police or public sympathy was spent on the crime, the money being the product of a property sale, and being spirited out of the UK to tax-exempt status in the Alps. The only way the owner could hope to get his money back was to 'come clean', admit hoarding and hope. But little hope was to be had: the notes were in large denominations, they were not marked, and although the notes were new and the serial numbers had been noted, the gang was clearly cautious and laundered the money patiently, using it to buy drinks in pubs up and down the country, or at bureau de change agents also up and down the country, changing five hundred pounds into used and untraceable American dollars or Swiss francs, which could then be paid into legitimate bank accounts. A large commission had been paid by the gang, either in currency exchange or the cost of an unwanted round of drinks, but at the end of a six-month period, the gang had obtained possession, it was estimated, of approx. 700,000 untraceable pounds. The gang had consisted of four persons, two large males, a small male and another small person who could be either male or female . . . the owner of the money being in a state of shock at the time was unable to give an accurate description. Payne was caught when he got careless. In many of the transactions, the gang had been careful to conceal their identity from CCTV cameras that were mounted in the bureaux de change, or on street corners near any pub they might use to buy a few drinks with a fifty pound note, or indeed from CCTV cameras inside any pub they might similarly use. Payne had just once let his shield drop, and one hot day he had gone into a bank, and asked to change a fifty pound note, against a clear policy of the gang. The bank clerk had become suspicious and had taken the note away, clearly to test for forgery or to check its number against wanted cash. Payne grew suspicious and anxious, had gripped the counter in front of the clerk's window and then fled, but not before he had left sixty seconds of footage of himself on the CCTV film. The quick-thinking clerk had then put a 'position closed' sign up in his window, thus deterring any subsequent customers from smudging the latents on the counter. The police were called and the Scenes of Crime officers lifted many fingerprints. One set was identified by the Police National Computer Database as belonging to James Payne. Payne, it transpired, had convictions for affray whilst he lived in London, had subsequently moved north and had not been known to the police for any reason until he tried to exchange a fifty pound note which he clearly knew to be 'hot'. Why else would he run out of the bank without his money? So reasoned the detective who wrote that section of the recording. Carelessness and panic . . . lucky for the police. If Payne had waited in the bank he could have said he had found the fifty pound note. Much suspicion would have been directed at him, but if he didn't crack under questioning, the police couldn't have taken their investigation of him any further, but by running, he signalled guilt. His E-fit and description were circulated, he was spotted in the street by a sharp-eyed constable who radioed for assistance, and Payne was arrested without a struggle. Once in custody, he admitted his part in the bullion robbery, and did so quite freely, as if relieved, so the recording noted, but wouldn't give details of his accomplices, nor of the location of the by then laundered money. Yellich could in a sense understand his reasoning: cough to it, do your time, hope for an early parole. When you come out you can walk down the street without looking over your shoulder, and you come out to a quarter share of seven hundred thousand pounds. If he lived out his life quietly, didn't throw the money about, and did nothing to draw attention to himself, then, yes, a few years bed and board at the expense of Her Majesty might indeed seem an attractive proposition. And he had hidden the money well: a search of his property revealed only documents pertaining to one bank account, with the National Westminster, with a balance of a modest £150. He also had a building society account with a £25 balance. The passbook of that account had been found in Pinder's small council flat, by which time the balance had increased to £100,000. So upon his discharge from prison after serving five of an eight stretch, Payne had re-flooded his account using his share of the stolen money, but that left another £100,000 unaccounted for. And that was just his share, assuming the gang had divided the proceeds equally.

Yellich put the file down. Once again that same gang appear, two large men, one small man, one short, stockily built woman. He picked up the file again, then consulted his notes. What he read made his scalp crawl. He reached for the phone on his desk.

Eric Filey left the pathology lab to answer the ringing telephone. He returned a moment later and said, 'It's for you, Chief Inspector.'

'Thank you.' Hennessey stepped forward and said, 'Excuse me' to Louise D'Acre who was clearly annoyed by the interruption. He walked to the anteroom, picked up the phone and said, 'Hennessey.'

'Yellich here, sir.'

'Yes . . . hope this is important, have you seen Dr D'Acre scowl? Never mind, what is it?'

'Greenwich, sir.'

'Yes.'

'Your roots are there, are they not?'

'Yes . . . very much so, never made a secret of it. Why?'

'Two streets, sir. Tyler Street and Tuskar Street, both in Greenwich.'

'Know them well.'

'Well, sir, I've just read the file on the bullion robbery which James Payne went down for.'

'Yes?' A note of curiosity entered Hennessey's voice.

'He lived at Tyler Street, Greenwich, when he was a teenager. He is, or was, about ten years older than Melita Campion, one of the four female students who went missing in York about twenty years ago.'

'Yes?'

'Well, her home address is Tuskar Street, Greenwich. Are they close to each other, those streets.'

'Close . . .' Hennessey gasped. 'They were practically next-door neighbours.'

Yellich replaced his telephone and sat back in his chair. James Payne (disappeared) and Melita Campion (murdered) had once been neighbours. And the description of that gang, the same description, two tall, well-built men, a small man, and a woman of stocky build, it keeps surfacing: it is the description given by drunkard Michael Henderson of the people responsible for the murder of the girl, it fits the description of James Payne and friends in whose house items of female clothing, some of which had belonged to Melita Campion, had been found, as if kept as trophies. It is the description of the gang who held up and robbed the man who was trying to smuggle £800,000 out of the UK. And it now transpires that Melita Campion and James Payne, victim and probable perpetrator, had once lived in adjacent streets in Greenwich, London. It seemed too much, too much, to absorb. He sat forwards, resting his elbows on the desk, and held his head in his hands. How, he thought, how could it be possible that this gang, which had clearly kept together for a number of years, had probably committed four murders, and a robbery . . . no . . . no . . . five murders, because the body of the man in Jeffrey Pinder's back garden was clearly a murder victim . . . how could they have evaded arrest? The police had caught one, James Payne, because of his carelessness, but he had not identified the others. However, even that didn't excuse it. Just very lucky or very clever. But in fairness to officers previously engaged in the disappearances of the four female students of twenty years ago, the gang could only now be linked to their vanishing, thanks to an alcoholic stumbling into the police station at the beginning of the week, wanting to get something off his mind. Yellich shook his head in wonder, just two and a half days into the investigation and they had linked five murders, and a bullion robbery, and had the name of one of the perpetrators and a description of the three others and a nickname, 'Izzy', for one of those three.

But some gang, some gang.

'So, what would you do?' The man leered at Yellich. He had difficulty in focusing. 'It's the only thing left . . . this.' He tapped the beer glass in front of him. 'How did you find me, anyway?'

'Criminal records.' Yellich sat opposite the man. 'Took a chance. I thought that a man who was capable of trying to spirit nearly a million pounds out of the country might be capable of doing other things that might earn him a place in our hall of fame.'

'And lo and behold.'

'Indeed.' Yellich looked around him. He liked the pub, quiet at present, lots of dark-stained wood, a solid bar, a gantry above the bar containing glasses, carpeted floor, round tables of wrought iron, stained-glass windows, some frosted windows too . . . tall ceilings, narrow corridors leading off and little snugs off the main corridor. A Victorian building, but the décor was replica, Victoriana, inside the real thing. 'Lo and behold.'

'You're lucky to catch me.'

'Oh . . . going somewhere?'

'In a sense. Six months to a year to live if I don't stop drinking.'

'That's what the doctor said?'

'Yes . . . and that was in the summer, early summer. I remember walking out of the surgery and seeing the crocuses popping up out of the soil and thinking lucky them, just starting out.'

Crocuses. Yellich remained silent but he thought April was the month for crocuses. If the doctor was correct, this leering, middle-aged man could be dead in a few weeks' time. He'll be lucky to make Christmas.

'I lost it all. Everything. I was forty years old, I had worked for twenty years.'

'Worked?'

'Well, ducked and dived, bobbed and weaved . . . put money here, put it there, got in at the right time. Money's like that, it attracts more money. I was just turned forty and I had a million smackers . . . then it was stolen from me, nothing to start over with.'

'But you stole it, in a sense.'

'Listen, sunshine –' the man eyed Yellich, his beer-induced leer had suddenly become a steely-eyed stare – 'I never stole nowt. Only took what was mine by right.'

'Some people wouldn't see it that way.'

'Oh, yes . . . like who?'

'Like the Inland Revenue. Had you paid your taxes in these twenty years of ducking and diving and bobbing and weaving, you would have had less than half of what was stolen from you. Not paying tax is a form of theft, but I don't expect you see it like that.'

'They got something . . . my house, what float I left in the bank . . . what cash I had in the house.'

'Which was a small percentage of what you owed.'

'Left me with nowt. I bet now.'

'Bet?'

'Horses . . . go dry for a few days, get a win, put it on an accumulator. Get a big win every so often, blitz it on the drink. That's been my life since I got robbed. I had a big house, indoor swimming pool, Roller in the garage . . . now I have a one-bedroomed council flat, the sort that nobody else wants . . . "hard to let" is the term. Don't pay rent on it, my neighbours do the same. We get threatening letters but we just tear them up. If we get evicted they just have to re-house us in the worst areas and since we are already in the worst area, there's no threat of eviction, so why pay rent?'

Yellich saw the logic in the man's argument, unethical as it was. 'So, what do you remember about it?'

'Everything. Despite this.' Again he tapped the glass. 'Can't remember what I did yesterday, but I remember the robbery . . . remember that. Often think I should have kept my mouth shut and just let the money go. It was only because I reported it that the Inland Revenue became interested, if I had let it go, I could have kept what I had left.'

'The house?'

'No, sold that, that was where the £800,000 came from. No, I had a bit left, enough to survive on . . . should have cut my losses. But I didn't think on . . . you investigating it again?'

'Possibly . . . possibly you can help us.'

The man leered again. The steely look was gone. 'I'm a Yorkshireman, born and bred – "Never do owt for nowt", that's the motto.'

'"And if you do, do it for thy sen."' Yellich finished the

'Yorkshireman's lament', so called. 'I'm born and bred as well.'

'So, it'll cost thee.'

'Oh, aye?'

'Aye . . . depending on what tha wants.'

'It'll help thee.' Yellich allowed himself to slip into broad Yorkshire – it seemed to aid communication – with: 'Might get thee thy brass back.'

'Aye?'

'Aye, happen it might.' Yellich raised an eyebrow. He now had 'divin' Dickie Mowatt's undivided attention.

'Straight up?'

'Straight up. See, if we recover it, the tax people will want what's theirs by right . . . owt left over is thine, by right.'

'If I had a bit of brass it would stop me drinking. I only drink because there's nowt else to do, but if I had a bit of brass I could start up again. You need brass to start up . . . more than I make on the horses.' Dickie Mowatt hadn't shaved for a few days, he wore a chequered-pattern shirt, an old leather jacket, dirty denims; heavy working boots helped him get between his 'hard to let' flat in Tang Hall across the river Foss to the Pack Horse Inn in old York down a secluded snickelway. And helped him get back again.

'Well, Dickie, help us, we help you.'

'You could buy me a drink, summat to be going on with, put me on that extra bit.'

'Could do, but I won't – it's killing thee, Dickie, so I won't.'

'Give us a tenner then.'

'No . . . it'll only go on drink for thee. If tha wants thy brass back, tha'll help us.'

'Alright.'

'I got the description of the gang . . . don't need that. What I want to know is, who knew you were carrying all that brass to Hull, and when and by what route?'

'That's what I wants to know. Told the police at the time, it had to be an inside job, but no one knew, no one I worked with. My lass at the time, she didn't know, never told no one.'

'OK . . . you lived alone in that big house.'

'Aye . . . my lass visited, stayed over a few nights at a time, but I didn't want marriage and kids, no nowt.'

'Nobody else in the house, secretary, typist?'

'No, I had an office in York for that, didn't put much on paper anyway, not my way. Liked to handle cash but I needed a business to help me.'

'Launder money?'

Dickie Mowatt shrugged. 'If you want.'

'Friends?'

'Up the golf club . . . but I was tight-lipped. I know how to keep my mouth shut.'

'What people did you see on a day to day, or week to week basis?'

'No one, just the people . . . no, wait. I used to have my house cleaned by a team of contractors . . . what did they call themselves? Oh, aye, remember, it was a team called Steps and Stairs.'

Yellich smiled.

'That little cow!' Dickie Mowatt shot to his feet, knocking his glass to the floor. The bar staff turned to him and Yellich anxiously. Yellich made an 'it's OK' gesture to them.

'What is it, Dickie? Remember something?'

'I do that.' Dickie Mowatt, sat down. 'I do that. It's taken all these years, but you just saying that . . . what you just said. That gang that forced me off the road, one of them a small, stockily built woman. I knew I knew her from somewhere . . . that walk . . . liked holding her arms out to balance herself, she cleaned my house, she was one of the Steps and Stairs team.'

Yellich stood and went to the bar as one of the bar staff appeared with a pan and brush to pick up the shattered pieces of Dickie Mowatt's glass. He bought Mowatt a pint of best bitter and stood it in front of him. He didn't think that one pint would make a deal of difference now. He also laid a ten pound note on the table in front of Mowatt. He didn't think that even a vast amount of drink would make any difference now, not to Dickie Mowatt.

Mowatt didn't respond. He stared blankly into space. He was 'away' somewhere probably, thought Yellich as he walked out of the pub, probably back in his large house with the indoor swimming pool and Rolls Royce in the garage . . . with a team of women cleaning and polishing and dusting, and now realizing that one of them was about to take him for £800,000 and set him on the path towards alcoholic dereliction and a 'hard to let' in Tang Hall.

Hennessey drove home. The post-mortem on the unknown male found buried in Jeffrey Pinder's back garden had concluded that death was due to multiple fractures of the skull. No other injuries were noted. As George Hennessey had requested, a photograph had been taken of the skull, the jaw had then been removed so as to facilitate identification by dental records, should a name for the deceased be forthcoming. Dr D'Acre had also removed a single tooth from the upper dentures to enable her to determine age at death of the deceased, plus or minus twelve months. She had also taken samples of marrow and hair to test for poison 'as a matter of course' though she had expressed the belief that the test would be negative. Hennessey had walked back through the city, unusually for him, because walking the walls was always his preferred option not just because of the aesthetics of walking medieval battlements, but also the sheer practicality of said practice. The walk, amid the early rush hour of jostling crowds, only served to reinforce the good sense of traversing the city via its walls. He strode casually up to Micklegate to the Bar at the junction with Blossom Street and into the Victorian, red-brick building that was Micklegate Bar Police Station. He signed out, went to the car park and drove home slowly at first as the rush-hour traffic congested the narrow roads, but acceptably quickly he was driving at a satisfying speed across flat landscape towards Easingwold and home.

Later that evening, Oscar having been fed and exercised, Hennessey packed an overnight bag and drove to a half-timbered house in Skelton. He always found Skelton a delightful village, with its tenth-century church. He parked outside a half-timbered 'L'-shaped house, walked up the gravel drive and was welcomed warmly into a house of family activity, of maths homework being done at one end of the long table that stood in the kitchen, whilst at the other, harnesses were being soaped and polished. Over the course of the evening, the shorter persons of the household seemed to disappear, going upstairs when all work that had to be done, whether for school or forthcoming horse show, had been. When calm had settled, only Hennessey and the lady of the house remained in the kitchen, sitting at the table looking affectionately into each other's eyes.

'It's gone quiet,' said Hennessey. 'Shall we go up?'

'Yes,' Louise D'Acre smiled. 'Let's go up.'

Seven

*In which the Chief Inspector travels to London
and to his roots and for the second time that
week, a member of the public gives information
about a recollection of an incident twenty years
earlier.*

THURSDAY, 11.00–22.00 HRS

'Paynes were never any good.' The elderly woman glanced out of her net curtains as she spoke. 'Not ever.'

Hennessey, listening, warmed to the homely familiarity of her east London accent and a part of him, just then, wished he had never left home. 'Knew them before James was born – his old man was in and out of prison and his old woman wasn't a deal better. Why, they in bother with the law again?'

'Possibly.' Hennessey relaxed in the armchair, relishing his surroundings. It wasn't the home he had grown up in, but the house was of identical design, even down to the stairs being on the left as one entered the house; the next-door house, Hennessey knew, would have stairs on the right as one entered it. 'James, anyway.'

'With the Yorkshire police? You know I've never been north of London in my life, never wanted to. Folk are different up country . . . harder . . . like the south, could hardly believe it when our Melita decided to go to York

164

to study. My man, Jack, that's his photograph there, he did all he could to warn her off, said he'd met northerners when he was in the army and he said it was true, they're aggressive, harder, violent and fight a lot. He said if there was ever a fight in the NAAFI, it would always be a few guys from the north and the Yorkshire boys were the worst of the lot. They seemed to like it, even the boys from Northumberland and Cumbria which are even further north than Yorkshire, weren't as violent as the Yorkshire men. That's what Jack said. We were so pleased when Melita wanted to go to university but not in the north country . . . oh, dear . . . she didn't want to go to London. We could understand that a young girl has to leave home, but the north? Why not Canterbury, we said, it's on the way to Ramsgate where we had our holidays each summer . . . not too far away, or Southampton? My Jack looked up all the universities south of London and showed them to her, but she was fixed in her mind. Never thought it would kill her though, and that was the end of Jack. He pined away, he took it bad, I mean really bad. She was our only one. I've felt like joining them from time to time. I've got a store of sleeping pills. I could have done away with myself at any time in the last twenty-four years. We knew she was dead.'

'You knew? Intuition?'

'Sixth sense, is that?' The woman was slightly built, frail, grey haired, wrapped in a red shawl but Hennessey sensed that inside she was made of steel.

'Yes.'

'No . . . she came to see us when she died. She looked so peaceful. That's how I know she's in heaven.'

Hennessey waited for the story he knew was coming.

'These houses have a small back garden, the kitchen looks out on to the back garden. I was in the kitchen and

165

I looked up and out of the window and our Melita was standing there . . . no clothes on . . . in the winter, but looking content. Jack came up and stood beside me as if he had been drawn to the window and we both stood in silence looking at our Melita . . . then she vanished. She came to say goodbye to us, you see. I looked at the clock, it was eighteen minutes past two in the afternoon. I took it off the wall and took the battery out and it's still there . . . still showing eighteen minutes past two. We talked about it, me and Jack, and Jack said that because she appeared naked to us, that meant she was naked when she died. That's the really upsetting bit, you know. That she was taken so young, that was bad enough, but it meant her end was horrible. So Payne did her . . . that's fate. The Paynes terrorized these streets, bad lot, so she goes away and writes to us that she met James Payne. Never thought he'd murder her. You didn't sound like a Yorkshireman.'

'I'm a Londoner.' Hennessey left it at that. He didn't tell Mrs Campion that each schoolday he walked past the end of that very street. There seemed to be no need.

Hennessey had caught an early train from York, a dark blue liveried GNER – 'the route of the Flying Scotsman', the train having started its journey that morning from Glasgow, calling at Edinburgh, Newcastle, Durham, Darlington and York, where George Hennessey boarded it. Three hours later at about 10 a.m. he'd stepped off the train on to the platform of the expansive canopy of Kings Cross Station, London. As always, he exited the station to say 'hello' to his native city, the red buses, the black taxis, and on that morning, thinking he had sufficient time to spare, he walked across the road to view St Pancras Station. He loved the edifice of St Pancras Station, the building being by far his favourite building . . . not just in

Britain, but globally, whether seen by his own eyes or only in print. Hennessey stood opposite the taxi rank, leaning against the wall which separated the station approach from the bustle of Euston Road below him and gazed in wonderment at the building, the graceful curve, the uncompromising Gothic architecture, the lovely brown colour of the stonework. Earlier that week he had seen old and very sophisticated carpentry and had had cause to be reminded of 'Pecker' the woodwork teacher, and now he was again reminded of his history teacher, who had once dismissed this beautiful building as 'the ugliest in Britain'. Oh, my, thought Hennessey in later years, how wrong you were. But having lived in Yorkshire for many years he now understood the sentiment, because his history teacher was a Lancastrian and therefore, he believed, a man of diminished responsibility. Having allowed his retina to be satiated with the awesome and inspiring vista of St Pancras's edifice, he entered the station, noticeably quieter than the bustling Kings Cross, and descended into the subway system, and the northern line to Charing Cross. From Charing Cross he took the overground to Maze Hill Station. From Maze Hill Station, he was on home territory, for this was Greenwich, the 'bottom end', on the way to Plumstead, not the 'posh end' up by the Naval College, the Maritime Museum, the Meridian and the *Cutty Sark*. In these streets he had grown up until he too, like Melita Campion, had left home. He'd found the Campion home on Tuskar Street and knocked on the door, having the previous evening telephoned Mrs Campion to ask if he could visit in connection with her daughter, Melita. He was warmly welcomed and a cup of tea was pressed on him by the elderly Mrs Campion who clearly wanted company, but more, much more, wanted to talk about Melita, to hear news, to receive information.

But the lady was insistent. 'What part of London?'

'Well, here, actually,' Hennessey was forced to concede. 'These very streets, just sheer coincidence that this investigation brought me back here, but I have visited when I can over the years.'

The woman eyed him, staring at him . . . Hennessey began to feel uncomfortable. 'George Hennessey,' she said.

'Yes . . .'

'Of Colomb Street . . . that Hennessey family?'

'Yes . . .'

'My father used to say, it's a small world and it gets smaller as you get older . . .'

'Do we know each other?'

'I'm not as old as I look, George . . . I've aged . . . I started to get old when Melita disappeared. I went grey overnight and started to walk with a stoop, I was only in my forties. This is . . . I don't have the words, I remember you at the junior school, before you went with all the other boys to Trafalgar Road School . . . it isn't there anymore . . .'

'I know . . . they pulled it down to make room for a block of flats.'

'Don't recognize me, do you?'

'I'm sorry?'

'Vera . . . my Christian name is Vera.'

'Vera . . . You are not Vera Swannell?'

The woman smiled. 'Inside, I'm the same Vera Swannell. We never had a lot to do with each other, you and me, George . . . different classes . . . different ages. In that time of life even one year is a big age gap, but I remember you – you and your mates knocked us off our hopscotch patch so you could play football with a tennis ball.'

'I remember that.'

'You'll have lunch with me?'

'No.' George Hennessey held up his hand. 'No, you'll have lunch with me, we'll eat out, on me.'

'Oh . . .' Vera Campion's eyes brightened. 'I haven't been out . . . and I have nothing to wear.'

'Whatever you feel comfortable in, but can we get back to the reason I have called?'

'Yes.' Vera Campion glanced at the small clock on her cluttered mantelpiece. 'But over lunch.'

'We're always told to report anything suspicious, I should have reported this twenty, nearly thirty years ago.' The man held eye contact with Yellich. He was middle-aged, corduroy trousers, sleeveless pullover, brown sports jacket, 'sensible' shoes, short hair, balding, clean shaven and, thought Yellich, quite trim for his years.

'Go on.' Yellich smiled. 'It's never too late.'

'Oh, but it is.' The man raised his eyebrows. 'That expression belongs in the rubbish bin with "everything happens for the best". It is often too late, and everything does not happen for the best. In this case if it is the same gang it is too late and everything has not happened for the best.'

'Accepted –' Yellich inclined his head – 'but what information do you have for us, Mr Chappell?'

'Heard the news last night, the regional news on television. The description of the gang wanted in connection with the murder of that girl . . . the skeleton that was found in waste ground out by Selby way . . . two large men, one small man, one girl.'

'Yes?'

'Perfect description of a gang that was in a pub once . . . the incident stays with me. I should have reported it then . . . the next day . . .'

'Well, tell me now.'

'I went out by myself for a beer . . . I used to do that in those days . . . stay at home now, most nights anyway. I got the yellow card shown to me by my doctor . . . anyway, in those days I'd just got divorced and had a lot of free time and a lot on my mind and I used to go for a wander by myself and invariably I would wander into a pub. Anyway, that night I wandered into the Handsome Beggar. I thought how appropriate, that's me just after being fleeced in the divorce settlement . . . a lonely beggar . . . and I stood at the bar and there was this group of four behind me, they were young and they fitted the description of the gang you want, fitted them to a T. It was what they said that made me notice them and remember them. See, the bar in the Handsome Beggar is an "L" shape, so I stood at the corner, looking down the bar, and they were to the left of the bar . . . got a really good view.'

'Tell me about them.'

'Descriptions?'

'Yes . . . well, the first guy, a big guy, overweight big, he was a real loudmouth and he spoke with a London accent. I mean east London.'

'Go on.'

'Second guy, he was also tall, but muscular, slim, he was also very handsome, put him in a dog collar and middle-aged ladies would swoon, but he looked very dangerous to me. You know "the devil can assume a pleasing form"? Well, that could have been written with him in mind. Just sat there, still, not saying a word, but watching, observing. I got the impression that the loudmouth was the gang leader, but the loudmouth would be nothing without the second guy. In fact there probably wouldn't be a gang at all without the second guy. The third guy was really small, really thin, barely five foot tall, I'd say. He was quiet too but he wore pointed shoes, "winkle-pickers" they used to be called – that pointed toe could give a vicious kick. I thought he looked as though he had a chip on his shoulder about being small. Hanging around two big guys like that couldn't have been good for his self image . . . and the fourth guy turned out to be a girl, sort of square shaped, wearing male-type clothing . . . jeans and boots . . . She too was quiet, never said a word, but what made them stand out, what made them stick in my mind is what they were saying, or what the big guy was saying. He said, and I quote, "We did a taxi driver last week and we hurt him bad" . . . and when they left they said, "We'll beat somebody up on the way home." Then they left the pub, the loudmouth first, the tall, slim guy second, the little guy with his winkle-pickers, and I could just see him going in with those shoes after the first two guys had decked someone, and the girl followed on, walking with a sort of jerky walk with her arms hanging outwards at her side, a bit like a penguin, I thought. I bet she would get her pound of flesh as well. I could visualize their action, the big two would deck someone then stand back while the small guy and the girl would put the boot in. When they had gone, me and another guy, who was clearly hearing what I was hearing, looked at each other and then away again, like as if we didn't want to hear it. Then I stayed far longer than I intended until they were well gone and then I slunk home . . . knowing that crew was on the town that night, I stuck to the bright lights and crowds as much as I could – usually I duck down a snickelway to cut a corner here and there, but not that night . . . the next day I just wanted to forget it . . . but soon I regretted not telling the police, all I had to have done was phone the police and say if someone gets done over tonight, or if a taxi driver was assaulted, seriously so, last week the gang that did it were in the Handsome Beggar and are known to the landlord.'

'They were known to the landlord?'

'Not in a friendly sense, didn't get the impression he liked them in his sawdust, but the loudmouth, he put the pint glass inside the inside pocket of his jacket, then raised his right arm up so as to bring the glass to his lips and he said, "New way of drinking it, Henry", or should I say, "'Enry" . . . "New way of drinking it, 'Enry". I did a bit of work for you, sort of compensated for not phoning the law like I should have done.'

'Oh, yes?'

'Called in at "the Beggar" last night. Landlord is still the same. "Henry Rule licensed to sell . . ." whatever licensees are licensed to sell – that was over the door. I went in and yes . . . it's the same bloke. Older now, as we all are, but the same fella. He could tell you about that gang, I'll bet, maybe names. All these years I thought they were getting their kicks from giving kicks, if you see what I mean, but after watching the news last night . . . if they went on from assaults to abducting and murdering women . . . well, perhaps I could have stopped it, if only I had made that phone call, if only, if only, if only . . .'

'If only,' Yellich echoed and reached for the statement pad. 'We'll probably never know, Mr Chappell, but at least you've come in now and what you have told us is promising. They sound like the felons we should be looking for – right description, right date, about . . . and the wrong attitude. And the connection with the Handsome Beggar. We'll take a stroll out there and have a chat with the landlord. I can always look it up in the *Yellow Pages*, but—'

'It's on Ousegate,' Tom Chappell interrupted Yellich.

'Small frontage – you could walk past it – but inside it's narrow and deep, hasn't changed . . . you'll see what I mean about the "L"-shaped bar. I was at the corner of the "L", they were round the first table to my left. I'm glad I came in, I feel better about myself, but I still should have reported what I heard at the time.'

'Well, yes and yes.' Yellich clicked his ballpoint and wrote the time and date at the top of the 'statement form'. 'Yes, I am pleased you came in, and yes, you should have reported it. You see, they still may not be the gang responsible for the four murdered women. My intuition says they are, but they may not be, so don't lose sleep thinking that you could have prevented these murders, but a police force is only as good as the information it receives and what you overheard that night should have been reported.'

'I see that now.' Tom Chappell nodded. 'I see it now.'

'I know she suffered, George.' Vera Campion looked up from her coffee and held eye contact with Hennessey. 'I know she suffered. A mother knows: appearing naked like that to her parents . . . she came to us when she died. Why would she be naked at that time of day, except doing something, being involved in something that would kill her? I know that young people, especially at university, take their pleasure during the daytime, but she was being murdered.'

'We don't honestly know, Vera.' Hennessey felt it diplomatic to keep from Vera Campion the inference of the six abrasions carved into the skirting board at the derelict house, of the derelict house itself, a lonely, lonely place to die, of the girl who secreted a small ballpoint into her mouth as a clue, hoping that someone, someday would find it. Four girls kept against their will, alone, knowing they were going to be murdered, and enduring who knows what degradation beforehand? 'Truthfully, we don't.'

Vera Campion forced a smile. 'You're not a good liar, George Hennessey, but I don't think I want to know what you know. I think I'd rather not know.'

They had lunched at the Last Viceroy on Trafalgar Road, each having a light lunch of a single course of curry, mild in both cases, lamb in his case, chicken in hers, and the conversation over the meal was of days gone by, what had happened to whom, and who had married whom, who had done well and who had fallen from grace. The meal time was not the time for discussion of solemn matters. It was when the second cup of coffee had been nearly completely drunk that Vera Campion had signalled that she was ready to return to the discussion of serious matters, by saying that she knew her daughter had suffered before she died, and probably as she died.

'That James Payne was involved,' she said grimly. 'I just know. He had a shop, you know.'

'No, I didn't know.'

'Yes, a little corner shop, in Holgate, York. She bumped into him. She was nineteen, he was about ten years older. Be in his fifties now . . . she walked in to buy something, and there he was behind the counter. They recognized each other immediately. She wrote and told me that same evening, "You'll never guess who owns our corner shop".'

'Well, well . . .'

'It was one of those shops that sells things that you run out of and can't go to the supermarket for such a small purchase, tea, coffee, milk, household items, newspapers, sweets for the children, and a jingly bell on the door which sounds as you push it open.'

'You visited?'

'Had to. Had to see where Melita had lived at the time she disappeared, had to collect her possessions from her room . . . visited the corner shop she told me about . . . wanted to tell Payne that I knew he was involved in Melita's disappearance and that I knew she was dead because she had come to see us . . . naked, when she died, but he wasn't there, just some small, weasely-looking boy with grinning, piercing eyes, eyes that said: I know something you don't know. He didn't give anything away but I think he knew who I was, and if he worked in the shop, he'd know Payne, and if he knew Payne, he would have known what happened to Melita. Women's intuition.'

'Did you tell the police?'

'I tried to do so, but you see it was still only a missing person then . . . not a murder until a body has been found. So now I am telling you again, that shop is the key to Melita's disappearance.'

'You know, you could very well be right there.'

'I am right.' Vera Campion drained her coffee cup. 'The girls in the house as good as said she disappeared after going to the shop.'

'They said that?'

'Not in so many words. They were staying for a drink at the university after lectures that day . . . one of them had something to celebrate, a birthday or something; Melita was invited to join them, they said, but she complained of a headache and said she was going to buy some headache pills and have an early night. You see, George, there were any number of places between the university and Holgate where she could have bought a packet of aspirin, but the chances are she would have bought them from Payne's shop, just before reaching home. Think about it,

George, a small shop, early evening, winter time, dark out, darker than London at five or six p.m. because you're in the north. She opens the doors, steps off the street – easy for someone as big as Payne to overpower her, if he had the little weasel-like geezer to help him, pull curtains over the shop door, lock the door, and turn the open/shut sign round to read "shut" . . . all over in a few seconds . . . he had a flat above the shop. As you went in you looked into a back room, an easy chair with the sound of a television, and between the counter and the backroom was a flight of stairs leading up to the flat. And you're telling me that Melita was one of the four girls who disappeared?'

'It looks that way, Vera, over an eight-year period . . . all students, but at different institutions, from different parts of the country, they were not connected . . . at the time. It's a trifle embarrassing for us now. You know, you could very well be right about that shop. The other girls, they too had addresses in YO26 – that's the Holgate postcode.'

'It was called "The Corner Shop", may even still be there . . . be under new ownership now – can't see Payne being a shopkeeper all these years.'

'He isn't. He did time for robbery.'

'Oh, good.'

'Only five years and out now, but for some reason wants us to believe he's dead.' And Hennessey told her about the body in Jeffrey Pinder's back garden and the statement that the body was that of James Payne.

'So who is the geezer in the ground?'

Hennessey raised his eyebrows. 'Just one more corpse to be identified.' He raised his hand and attracted the waiter's attention. 'I'll need a photograph of Melita,' he said, reaching for his wallet, 'taken as close to her disappearance as possible.'

'I can let you have the very last photograph taken of her, about a few weeks before she died.'

'That would be excellent. We can use it to confirm her identity.'

'Can you?'

'I won't tell you how, it's a bit grisly.'

'I can cope.'

'Well, they superimpose a photograph of her on to a photograph of the skull and match up points like the cheekbones and the eye sockets, and jaw line, and if they fit, it's deemed a positive identification.'

'That's not grisly.'

'You're a strong woman, Vera.'

'Now I just want to live long enough to see Payne convicted. After all these years, something is finally happening.'

'All started on Monday of this week when a drunkard came into the station . . . it had taken him twenty years to recollect something. That started the ball rolling.' Hennessey reached for his wallet and dropped his credit card on the bill, which the waiter whisked away with practised smoothness.

'What was it he told you?'

'Now that I won't tell you.'

'Bad?'

'Bad enough. Can you tell me who Melita's dentist was?'

'Mr Dent, on Trafalgar Road, Mr Dent, the dentist. Retired now. New geezer in now.'

'Thanks . . . we can also confirm identity from dental records, if they have been kept. A dentist has to keep them for eleven years, after that he can dispose of them . . . but a new dentist has taken over, twenty years on.'

'Twenty-four . . .'

'Sounds like we'll be depending on the photograph.'

'You'll be dashing off then?'

'I'll have to, pay a call to Colomb Street.'

'Yes, George . . . I was sorry about Graham . . .'

'Yes, thanks . . . we have both had our tragedies, and I want to get back to St Pancras before dusk.'

'Really? Why?'

So Hennessey told her about his passion for the building.

Yellich walked from Micklegate Bar down Micklegate, across the bridge and into Ousegate, where the ancient blended with the modern. To his right the city was very ancient and there stood St Peter and St Paul Passage, being one of York's snickelways. He turned into the passage, wide enough for two people to pass if they slide sideways to each other, and low enough for a tall man to reach the roof. The passage bent sharply twenty feet in from the main thoroughfare and led on to a building set in the buildings, with small bay windows of frosted glass, flowers in wooden tubs beneath and a door of gloss black. A sign above the door read: 'The Handsome Beggar est 1790 AD.' Quite young, thought Yellich, as he approached the door, quite young for one of the old pubs. Inside, the beams were low, the carpet dark, the tables dark stained, but the atmosphere was warm, comfortable, homely. A little natural light crept in through the frosted glass of the bay windows but the main source of light was artificial. Like casinos, albeit unintentionally, the separation from natural light also encourages a separation from reality, encouraging punters to stay, encouraging them to part with their money. Modern pubs deliberately strive for the effect, but the Handsome Beggar had had the effect for over two hundred years. The bar was indeed 'L'-shaped, as Tom Chappell had described. Yellich stood at the bar at a point which corresponded to the corner of the 'L' and glanced at the first table to his left, presently unoccupied. If the pub had not been refurbished in the last twenty years, and if Tom Chappell's information was truthful and accurate, then at that table had once sat the gang of four, now sought for a series of murders, four women and one man. It made Yellich feel tantalizingly close to his prey. A young man in a white shirt and tie approached him and smilingly asked, 'Can I help you, sir?'

'Oh, I hope so.' Yellich flashed his ID. 'Is the landlord here?'

'It's a managed pub, sir.' The young man had a badge which said his name was 'Toby' and that he was 'here to help'. That alone, Yellich reproached himself, that alone should have told him that the Handsome Beggar now belonged to a chain.

'The manager then.'

'I'll ask him to come to see you, sir.'

Yellich nodded his thanks and Toby walked keenly away. Yellich glanced round the room. One man sat alone reading a tabloid, the other people in the room were a couple who leant close to each other but each of whom wearing a stern expression as if at the stage of talking to each other again after a mother and father of a row, which had probably been brewing for months.

'Can I help you?' The manager wasn't a deal older than Toby, in Yellich's eyes.

'Well . . .' Yellich said, and thought 'probably not' as his heart sank upon seeing the tender age of the manager. Whatever this infant might recall from twenty years ago would be of doubtful interest to the police. 'I'm actually making enquiries about a gang of punters who came in here twenty years ago and was hoping to speak to the landlord. I was told it was a Mr Rule . . . I was clearly misinformed . . . yet the name on the sign?'

'No misinformation, sir. Henry's still with us – different designation. The company bought the "Beggar" from the brewery; it's a free house now but Henry was kept on because of his expertise. He moved from being a landlord to a manager, but the same bloke does the same job. He can run this pub blindfolded, and the name over the door, that's company policy, gives the impression of being a tenanted pub belonging to a brewery. The market-research people say the customers prefer that in old pubs of cities. The customers are happy with pubs that belong to a chain in new development areas or in converted buildings, but pubs as old as this have to give the impression they are still pubs in the traditional sense. But Henry's here – I'll ask him to come and see you, sir.'

He too turned and walked keenly away, leaving Yellich with the impression that whichever company 'Toby' and the youthful manager worked for, it was a company that standardized both the speech and the body movements of its employees. But when, a few moments later, Henry Rule appeared, he proved himself to be a man of the old school. He shambled towards Yellich wearing corduroy trousers and a yellow cardigan over a blue, open-necked shirt. 'Aye?' he said.

'Here to pick your brains, Mr Rule.' Yellich smiled.

'Pick away, if you can find any – they've been thoroughly marinated now.'

So Yellich picked, and he did not have to pick very far before Henry Rule said, 'The gang of four mentioned on the news? About those four bodies just dug up? I did wonder.'

'You know who I am talking about?'

'Oh, aye . . . I know alright.' Henry Rule set his jaw firm. 'I know alright.'

'Seen them lately?'

'No. Not for a few years . . . a pub has its regulars, but a city centre pub has regulars for a few years only. Out in the suburbs a pub will have regulars who have been coming for twenty years, more, but in the city, regulars go in short spells and the gang you're interested in belonged to a different era. They were regulars about . . . see . . . about the time my youngest was born . . . he was a late baby . . . quite unexpected . . . he's now twenty-two, final year at Newcastle University . . . he was born about the time they used to come in.'

'Know their names?'

'Payne . . . James Payne, he was the leader . . . noisy character, from East London, but south of the Thames he once told me . . . Greenwich, I think he said. Well-built lad, another called "Izzy", he was fairly quiet, had a serious side to him though.'

'Izzy,' Yellich repeated. 'That's a nickname . . . do you know his real name?'

Henry Rule rested two meaty forearms on the counter. Even concealed inside the cardigan Yellich could tell they were barrel-like . . . the slow, masculine way he moved. 'Izzy,' he said, looking round the bar in thought . . . the wood panelling, the duplicates of ancient maps favoured by York licensees . . . the couple still in earnest conversation, the flashing lights of the fruit machine. 'Ismay,' he said at length, 'yes, that's his surname . . . David "Izzy" Ismay.' Yellich smiled and took out his notepad. He wrote David "Izzy" Ismay on a fresh page. 'They were a gang of four?'

'Yes, another guy, small, he had a chip on his shoulder, and a girl . . . in fact you'll know both of them.'

'We will?'

'Yes . . . the girl . . . she got the chop from the Welfare Department, she had a job helping out old folk, helped herself to their cash . . . got this from James Payne. Payne, you see, he would always assume I was on his side, let them drink in here. I didn't like them but they never did anything to have me scratch them for it. Payne thought that meant I liked him. He was buying a round one time, the girl was looking angry, like someone had done her a bad turn and the others were buying her drink . . . trying to make her feel better about herself. Anyway, Payne comes to the bar, elbows a couple of other punters out of the way and drops a load of shrapnel on the bar. They were never wealthy you see, always counted pennies . . . not wealthy in those days anyway. I read in the *Post* how Payne got time for robbery . . . a lot of dosh as well.'

'Enough,' said Yellich. 'But the woman?'

'Oh, aye . . . Payne told me she was chopped because she had been helping herself to an old lady's money. Payne said, "The silly cow got greedy," as if I was sympathetic to her . . . as if I should want a woman like that in the pub. But Payne was like that . . . she had a name . . . similar to the old lady's name . . . can't remember her surname, did get to know it, but her first name was Dorothy.'

'Dorothy.' Yellich wrote in his pad. This, he felt, was proving to be a most fortuitous visit. 'And the guy?'

'The small guy . . . I didn't like him. Didn't like any of them but didn't like him especially. Nasty piece of work. Now, what did they call him? Had a name that fitted him like "Little" or "Short", or something like that . . . "Small", that was it . . . Tim Small, "Tiny" Tim Small.'

'And we'll know him as well, you think?' Yellich added 'Tiny' Tim Small to the list.

'Yes . . . small stuff, youthful still, breach of the peace, drunk and disorderly, but I got the impression that small as he was he was a clever little devil. I felt he was getting away with more than he was getting done for. You get to know people in this business . . . it's really a people business . . . and him, I've met the type before – get done for parking on yellow lines but get away with murder.'

'Funny you should say that,' said Yellich, closing his notebook.

'Those four women?' Henry Rule held eye contact with Yellich. 'So it was that gang?'

But Yellich just raised his eyebrows. 'Thank you for your time and information,' he said, and turned and left the pub.

Hennessey walked Vera Campion back to her house, and accepted her invitation of a cup of tea before returning 'up country'. Hennessey stood beside her in the kitchen as she looked out over her small back yard.

'Just there,' she said, 'by the fence, on the path just this side of the shed. She stood there . . . naked as the day she was born, but she was a woman then, of course. We watched her. She seemed to know when to go, when we had both seen her and when we both knew the significance of what we were witnessing . . . then she vanished. But she was there alright: one might have been seeing things, imagining it . . . the mind plays tricks . . . but two . . . we turned to each other, me and him and he said, "She's gone, she came to say goodbye." After that I watched him age by the day. It was like he put a year on each week . . . soon I was by myself. Will you brew the tea while I look for that photograph you asked for?'

Later, Hennessey left Vera Campion's house after she

insisted on hugging him and making him promise to keep in touch. He readily agreed to do so but doubted it would be more than a card-each-Christmas manner of keeping in touch. He walked down Tuskar Street into Trafalgar Road, busy as ever he had recalled it, too narrow for the volume of traffic it was expected to carry, and then turned right into Colomb Street, to the front door of a little terraced house. He stood looking at it where, below, in the kerb, Graham would spend hours polishing his beloved silver and chrome motorbike, and on Sundays Graham would take him on the pillion, up Trafalgar Road, round by the *Cutty Sark*, over the Thames by Tower Bridge, round Trafalgar Square, back across the river by Westminster Bridge, back to Greenwich . . . then one night . . . Hennessey looked up at the front upstairs window, the window of the room that had been his bedroom, hearing Graham kickstart the machine as he lay in bed, aged about eight or nine years . . . listening to his brother drive the machine away, straining to catch every last decibel of the two-stroke roar until it faded in the night, to be replaced by other sounds – ships on the river, the Irish man, drunk, walking up Colomb Street towards the Vanbrugh Tavern, reciting his Hail Marys . . . Then the knock on the door, tap, tap . . . tap . . . the urgent conversation, his mother's wailing, his father coming to his room to tell him that Graham had ridden his bike to heaven 'to save a place for us'. And the funeral . . . a summer funeral. So odd, his brother's coffin going down into the ground as birds sang and butterflies fluttered . . . it was so wrong somehow – people shouldn't die in the summertime, he thought. Graham had gone in the summer and then a little over ten years later, Jennifer too had gone in the summertime . . . winters are for funerals . . . summers should be for weddings and christenings and things joyous. After that there had been a gap in his life, a constant gap, a void where there had once been someone to follow. And he had always disliked motor vehicles. He could never understand folk's passion for them, whether two wheels or four, they were, he believed, the most dangerous machine ever invented. He turned and walked up Colomb Street to Mazehill Station and arrived at St Pancras Station in time to see the red brickwork glow becomingly in the setting sun.

'We were just starting out,' said the woman, 'we had difficulty attracting staff.' She looked embarrassed. 'Now, of course, we would vet each applicant, especially since we clean inside people's houses as well as commercial premises.'

'Of course.'

'But Dorothy Hodges . . . she was a disaster.'

'Hodges,' Yellich wrote in his notebook.

'She came to us without any employment history, so she said. Now of course we see that as suspicious. She said she'd been living in Greece for the last few years, making a living sketching folk on the beach . . . that was her story.' The woman seemed to Yellich to be in her fifties, behind her were framed photographs of yellow 'Steps and Stairs' vans. The office was well appointed, with potted plants, tinted glass looking out over the Ouse. Steps and Stairs had clearly thrived over the last twenty years. 'She wasn't particularly good at the job, not really diligent enough, but, like I said, we needed staff. The early days were difficult – we nearly collapsed a few times.'

'Did you ask for a reference?'

'Yes . . . and she provided one, bogus as it turned out, but bogus references are easy to get, just a couple of lines: "Ms Hodges was a cleaner in my house, I found her competent and trustworthy", something along those lines.'

'How long was she with you?'

'Five years before we tumbled her . . . chance conversation it was. York being a small city, I was chatting to a friend, not a close friend, an acquaintance who works in the city's welfare department who told me about a home help who was sacked once for stealing from one of her clients . . . they call them clients. The story was that this woman was a home help for an elderly lady who was almost totally blind. They had similar names – I think it was that that triggered the home help thoughts . . . and she lifted one of the old lady's cheque books and started using the cheques to purchase things, usually by mail order, accepting that she would have to wait until the cheque cleared. The elderly lady was very wealthy, I should tell you. Anyway her son visited and checked his mother's bank statements and realized there should be more money in the account than was shown in the statement. He noticed valuables appeared to be missing from the home, so he went to the police. The police had difficulty tracing the person who was writing the cheques, but for the fact that a pattern emerged. Every so often a cheque was made payable to a ladies' hairdressers, the same hairdresser, so the police went to see the hairdresser and asked her if they knew of a customer called Mrs Diana Hodgeson. They said yes, said she was a youngish woman who came in to have her hair done about once a month, and the police said, "She's not, you know, she's well into her seventies, blind as a bat and can hardly walk." So the police asked the hairdresser to let them know the next time Mrs Diana Hodgeson made an appointment, which they did. The police sent along two plain-clothed female officers, who sat there looking like customers whilst this woman had her hair done. They waited until she paid by cheque, they accepted a cheque from her without a credit card because she was a known customer, then they pounced. Turns out the woman was called Dorothy Hodges . . . it was then that I sat up. I asked my friend to describe her. She couldn't, never having seen her, just heard the story from one of Hodges' colleagues in the Welfare Department. I asked her if she could get a description to me. She did the next day. I said, "My heavens, that woman works for me. No wonder she didn't give an employment history and I have been sending her to folk's houses." So I confronted her with it and she admitted it. She claimed she had not let Steps and Stairs down but it was the only way she could get a job. Then she just walked out without me telling her she was fired. I think she took the old lady for thousands, and I mean thousands, plus valuables, but she could only be prosecuted for the half dozen cheques she had written to the hairdresser.'

'You have no record about her?'

'No . . . we didn't keep files on our staff once they had left us . . . Now we do . . . but in those days . . . I sent her cards to her and then binned the file and the bogus reference along with it.'

'Remember her address?'

'No . . . not specifically, but it was in Holgate.'

'I understand that you used to clean the house of a man called Mowatt? Richard, "Dickie" Mowatt . . .'

'Mr Mowatt . . . yes, he was a good customer. He went bankrupt when he was robbed . . .' The woman's voice tailed off and she visibly paled.

Yellich nodded. 'Dorothy Hodges was a small stocky woman . . . probably still is?'

'Yes.'

'I saw Mr Mowatt just yesterday. He remembers one

187

of the gang that robbed him by forcing his car off the road, but he couldn't place her until yesterday. Suddenly he was able to place her by her walk . . .'

'Sort of rocked from side to side with her arms out-stretched a bit . . . about at forty-five degrees to her spine. Yes, she had a distinctive walk alright . . . So, she robbed him . . . she did let us down.'

'Quite significantly I'd say. I don't think she stole any valuables from Mr Mowatt, but she certainly found out he was going to be carrying a vast amount of cash and on what route, on what day . . . probably she overheard a telephone conversation . . . told her friends, and they followed him. Do you recollect anything at all about her private life?'

'I don't think she mentioned anything, not to me . . . but I wasn't one of the cleaning team. She probably would have chatted to them as they drove from job to job . . . but none of them are with us now . . . we have a very high turnover of staff . . . cleaning other people's houses is not a job that has appeal. It offers unskilled employment to women, and one or two men over the years, but they never stay long. I can understand that.'

'I see. Never mentioned anyone called James Payne?'

'No.'

'Or "Izzy"? David "Izzy" Ismay?'

'No.'

'Or "Tiny" Tim Small?'

'Again, no. They being her friends?'

'Yes . . . a gang of four that we are anxious to have a chat with. They'll be in their late forties, early fifties by now.'

'She never mentioned those names, but like I said, I never really spoke to her. Well . . . well . . . I never . . . this has come into my life like a bombshell.'

*   *   *

Hennessey thought it had been a good day, an astounding day on a personal level, but a day which moved the case along. He sat in a forward-facing seat of the GNER east coast mainline express as it sped north through Hertfordshire in fading light. He was in possession of a photograph of Melita Campion taken only a month before she died, fuller faced with teeth showing and thus more useful than the one already in the 'mis per' file which he was confident could be matched to one of the skulls . . . thus allowing an old school chum to lay her daughter to rest . . . to have a grave to visit, a headstone to talk to. He could link the man James Payne to her, by his little corner shop, into which Melita Campion had probably entered to make her last purchase in life. He also thought that Vera Campion's notion of any young woman being in danger if she walked into a small shop, should the shopkeeper be of criminal intent, was fair and reasonable. So fair and reasonable that he felt he would not be able to look at corner shops in the same way again. He was also in possession of information, which could not be admitted in court but might be allowed to assist the police, that Melita Campion was naked when she died at eighteen minutes past two on a winter's afternoon. He settled back in the seat, the train was due in at York at 9 p.m. . . . time to get to Easingwold, feed and exercise Oscar and stroll into town for a pint of stout at the Dove Inn. A perfect way to end a very productive day. And something to share with DS Yellich upon the morrow, he thought.

Yellich too felt it had been a very, very good day. He was pleased with the information he had uncovered. He now had the names of the members of the gang who appeared to have been responsible for the murder of at least one of the four young women, and three of the four

189

were reported to be known to the police. The net was closing. He walked back to Micklegate Bar Police Station reaching it about 5 p.m. He checked his pigeonhole – there were messages from the Derbyshire police, the Liverpool police and the Somerset and Avon police, each indicating that photographs of Charlotte Philips, Christine Tate, and Joyce Bush respectively, were being sent by courier to Micklegate Bar for his attention. At his desk he picked up the phone and dialled the collator's office, requesting all information on Dorothy Hodges, Timothy Small and David Ismay to be located, also for his attention. He took the file and added an account of his visit to the Handsome Beggar and Steps and Stairs. He left the police station at six, drove home to a warm welcome by his loving wife and his loving son, a peaceful night in, an early bed thinking of what 'gold dust' he was able to share with DCI Hennessey, also on the morrow.

Eight

In which a house of cards collapses and George Hennessey revisits Greenwich and his old school friend.

FRIDAY, 08.30–17.30 HRS

It was a pleasing sight. Both Hennessey and Yellich thought it was a pleasing sight. Both men had retired to bed the previous night feeling the intense satisfaction of a good day's work having been done and in the case of Hennessey, a day of some personal satisfaction. Both had slept soundly, both had awoken refreshed after a solid sleep, both had been eager to arrive at Micklegate Bar Police Station to share gleaned information with the other. This they did enthusiastically over coffee in Hennessey's office. Further developments occurred in the form of photographs of Charlotte Philips, Christine Tate and Joyce Bush, having arrived by courier from disparate parts of the UK and having been sent on forthwith to the forensic science laboratory at Wetherby for possible matching with the skulls of the skeletons that had been unearthed from the waste ground on Monday and Tuesday of last week. Yet further progress was afforded by the collator providing files on David Ismay, Tim Small and Dorothy Hodges: each had a recent address, none had been 'active' criminally speaking for fifteen years, save Payne, who alone had been convicted of the robbery

191

of Richard Mowatt. Interestingly, none of the gang of four had convictions that linked him or her to any of the others.

'They were lone operators as well as coming together to do big jobs,' Hennessey remarked, reading the track of each one's previous convictions. 'And nothing for some time . . . burnt-out psychopaths. It will happen apparently.' Hennessey drained his mug of coffee and replaced it on a sheet of scrap paper which had long served as a coaster, given the half circles of coffee stains it had accumulated. 'If a psychopath is not caught, he'll burn out and stop killing. This lot were a gang of four, they murdered together and burnt out together. But shared loyalty to each other. Payne didn't grass up his mates . . . Pinder was prepared to sit on a dead body in his back garden and pretend it was Payne.'

'Loyalty or greed, boss.' Yellich raised his eyebrows. 'I mean, Payne keeping schtum meant the money was there when he came out – that dosh was never recovered. You can buy a lot of silence with that type of money. Any psychopath I have ever met has always been out for himself, or herself. They'll shaft their friends if they think it will profit them. Frankly I can't see Payne having any high moral qualities like loyalty, never having met him, of course.'

Hennessey pursed his lips. 'Not having met him either, I think you are right. I was being too generous-spirited with my assessment.'

'So, what do we do now, boss – bring them in for a quiz session?' Yellich leaned forward and placed his similarly empty mug on Hennessey's desk. 'Once they're all collared, they'll start squealing like stuck pigs . . . wanting to plea bargain.'

'You think so?'

'Out for themselves, as we said.'

'Yellich, you disappoint me. They are all guilty of abduction, false imprisonment, who knows what degradation of those women and murder, five counts, and that's what we know . . . as with all criminals there's crimes committed by them that we don't know about. Also three of the gang, and possibly Pinder, are involved in the robbery. It may be more than twenty years on now, they may well have burned out, they may well be settled in late middle-age with steady jobs, a family even . . . but they are going down for life. There's no plea bargaining to be had for them, and they'll know it, they'll also know we are closing in. They'll have read the newspapers, watched television, they'll know the bodies have been discovered, they'll know Pinder's been lifted. When we move, we have to have evidence. You remind me of the story of the two lions . . . have you heard it?'

'Don't think so, boss.'

'Two lions, an old one and a young one, they're lying in the grass looking into a valley where a herd of antelope are grazing. The young lion says, "Let's dash down there and between the two of us we can grab one." The old lion says, "No . . . no . . . let's creep down there and grab the lot."'

Yellich smiled. 'Nice one, boss . . . so, which way do we creep?'

'Well, there's two places I would like to creep. I think the first place is YO26.'

'Payne's shop?'

'Yes . . . it seems to be the scene of the abduction. My old school friend was quite correct – small shops are very dangerous if they're staffed by persons of criminal intent.'

'Like Payne and his gang?'

'As you say . . . I can picture it, sadly – Melita Campion popping into the corner shop, thinking she's safe because she knows Payne from home, doesn't like him but he's familiar . . . and thinking she's safe because there are other people in the shop . . . and one is a woman. Someone comes in behind her . . . switches the open/shut sign round . . . and suddenly the people in the shop pounce and bundle her upstairs. She's restrained, silenced with a gag or a knockout potion . . . or threats, because a gag won't stop you making noise. It'll stop you enunciating words but you can still kick up a heck of a row, even with a piece of cloth stuffed into your mouth . . . but she's silenced, the shop is re-opened and goes on trading until closing time. All over in thirty seconds.'

'Frightening. I'll never look at corner shops in the same way again.'

'I thought the same thing yesterday.'

'Do the same thing four times over eight years, who will suspect the corner shopkeeper? They may even have targeted their victims, getting to know them, making sure they didn't get two lassies from the same college. I'd like to see that shop. I'd like to creep there in the first instance. Then I'd like to creep over to Full Sutton, have a little talk with Pinder . . . watch the colour drain from his face as he realizes he is in much more deeply than unlawful disposal of the dead. If we can link him to the murders in any way . . . at the moment we can only link him to Payne . . . but if we can link him to the murders he's looking at life in the slammer as well. There's a story to be told there . . .'

'There is, isn't there? The story told by Pinder, it just doesn't ring true.'

'Remind me of what he said.'

'Did work for Payne, home visit to repair the Citroën,

went walkabout round the house, half-inched some ladies' underwear . . . it turned him on. What he had pinched was clothing Payne had kept as trophies from the murdered women. Payne came demanding the clothing back, there was a fight, Payne took second prize . . . Pinder panicked and buried him in the garden. But whoever the body in the garden is, it isn't James Payne.'

'Pinder's got some explaining to do.'

'Alright . . . no time for guessing. Let's creep down into YO26, check that shop, then we'll creep over to Full Sutton.'

Yellich stood. 'My car, boss?'

'Of course.' Hennessey also stood. 'You know how I hate driving.'

'Took over from James Payne, love.' The present proprietor of the Corner Shop was a gruff-spoken, thickset, silver-haired man, long-sleeved green pullover, jeans. 'Been here since . . . looking for a buyer . . . want my retirement money. I'll sell it . . . it's a little goldmine, love, this little shop.'

'What sort of people shop here?'

'All sorts, love.' The man changed a plug as he spoke. 'Local folk, students . . . a lot of students . . . they rent houses round here, love. I've got a couple of tenancies, I rent out . . . nice little earner that.'

Hennessey considered the layout of the shop. The door was covered on the inside with a fly screen of myriad coloured strands presently fastened down the one side allowing the owner to see out of the glass door of the shop, but which could be allowed to hang vertically at an instant and so prevent anybody seeing the inside of the shop from the street. The door of the shop faced the solid brick wall of the end house of a terrace across the street. The shop door thus could not be overlooked, save by a pedestrian who might happen to be passing. A sentry posted outside the shop could easily alert any conspirator within to the approach of a member of the public who may observe an abduction. Inside the shop a hinged section of the counter directly opposite the door would allow an abductee to be forced to the other side of the counter. Beyond the counter, as Vera Campion had said, was a rest area. Hennessey could see an armchair, and a television was to be heard, at the moment tuned into an Australian soap opera. Between the rest area and the shop area, also as Vera Campion had described, was a set of stairs which led up to the flat above the shop. Opposite the stairs was another doorway, which led out to a small garden with a lush privet hedge around it, at the side of the shop, and to the kerb. An easy route by which to take an overpowered, restrained young woman from the shop to a waiting car, at the dead of a winter's night, for onward transportation to the derelict eighteenth-century house at the edge of a piece of wasteland, out in the country, out on the way to Selby. Hennessey knew why Vera Campion had visited the shop. He also knew there was little point in asking to visit the upstairs flat – there would be no trace of any abductee, not after this length of time.

'You'll be getting a pension, love.' The shopkeeper screwed the plug together.

'Sorry?' Hennessey said.

'You'll be getting a pension . . . you'll be close to it, you look about my age. I won't go early like police officers, I have to sell this shop to get a pension . . . got my tenancies though . . . but I want a good lump sum. I've worked hard enough, love, always a shopkeeper.'

'Did you know James Payne at all?'

'Hardly at all. Enough to know he wasn't a shopkeeper . . .

wrong attitude . . . a bit of a flash Harry . . . a little corner shop wasn't him. He went from this into selling booze – that was more him. Read he got done over for theft, big case a few years ago now, took a bloke for nearly a million quid . . . now that really was him. My wife said he made her shudder. Had friends as well, helped him move out as we were moving in . . . a shifty looking crew.'

'Really?'

'Yes . . . three guys and a small woman . . . avoided all eye contact . . . really cleaned the house out, took everything, carpets, curtains, smelled like the place had been cleaned with bleach, really scrubbed it.'

'That's interesting.' Hennessey glanced to his right. The shop extended only a few yards to the further wall . . . goods on shelves, a walk space, then the counter. Nowhere to escape to once Payne and his gang started to close in. 'Three guys, you say?'

'Sure it was three?' Yellich echoed.

'Yes. Tall good-looking guy, one very small, and another sort of in between.'

'Remember any names?'

'No, sorry . . . it was a long time ago.'

'They left nothing at all behind them?'

'No, nothing. Had to fit it all from scratch – cost a lot of money . . . Mind you, talk about leaving something behind, there is an atmosphere in the flat . . . in the front room particularly and she refused to live here. It was the last straw – things had been bad between us for a while and were not going to get better. Soon after we moved in, she moved out and started divorce proceedings. I carried on by myself.'

'Have you felt the bad atmosphere?'

The shopkeeper scratched his cheek. 'I'm not as sensitive about things like that as Linda was . . . but . . . I don't feel comfortable in the room – strange sensation of being watched, and I can't heat the room . . . No matter how much I turn up the fire I can't make the room warm, so I only really use it in the summer. I have a bedroom upstairs and this room behind me here. When I shut the shop up for the night, I stay downstairs in that room, watching television, then I go up to my bed. Only use the front room in the summer.'

'How long did Payne own the shop before you bought it?'

'About ten years. So I believe. Before that it was owned by a fella called Robinson – he and his wife ran it. Before them, I don't know.'

'It's alright,' Hennessey said, 'we are really only interested in Payne and his friends.'

'Weird lot, like I said . . . and local people said it was good when they sold up . . . It was never a happy shop . . . so folk told me, never welcoming. I suppose he found out the hard way that he wasn't cut out for shopkeeping, not a small corner shop, anyway.'

Outside Hennessey and Yellich viewed YO26: streets of smooth cobble, dark, stained terraced houses in rows.

'Alright –' Hennessey turned to Yellich – 'let's creep on to Full Sutton.'

The three men sat in the agent's room. The same room in which Yellich had interviewed Pinder earlier that week. The cream-coloured walls, the pane of opaque glass set high, the steel table bolted to the floor, the steel chairs, sitting freely on the floor but not designed for comfort.

'I'll tell you what we know, Jeffrey,' Hennessey said as Yellich offered Pinder a cigarette and lit it for him. 'We know that you are linked to Payne and his gang. How do we know that? We know that because the body you buried in your garden isn't James Payne.'

'So you lied to us about that,' Yellich said as Pinder's eyes widened, then narrowed.

'We'll want to know who that is, but we'll come back to that,' Hennessey continued. 'We know four young women were murdered over an eight-year period about twenty years ago, and that they were probably abducted when they popped into Payne's little shop to buy something.' Pinder began to look worried. He began to fidget, began to look at the floor, then at the wall.

'We know the names of the gang: James Payne, Tim Small, David "Izzy" Ismay and Dorothy Hodges.'

'And you, Jeffrey,' added Yellich. 'It wasn't a gang of four all along, it was a gang of five.'

'Four people helped Payne remove from his flat . . . you fit the description of the fourth. The shop is still in the hands of the gentleman Payne sold it to, he'll pick you out of an ID parade. We also know from information we can't use of a supernatural nature, like appearances of the dead to their loved ones and rooms which can't be heated, that at least one of the four young women was murdered in the front room of the flat above the shop. That was probably Melita Campion. I think that because she was naked when she died, the others were kept alive in a derelict house in winter . . . they would have been allowed clothing to stay alive.'

Yellich remained silent. Michael Henderson had described a young woman being dragged naked across the waste ground to a shallow grave. He knew that in all probability all four women had been naked when they died. But Hennessey was probing. He remained silent, never taking his eyes off Pinder, and let Hennessey probe.

'We also know that Payne's gang were responsible for the robbery . . . Nearly a million pounds was taken from a fellow called Mowatt . . . and you were part of that.'

'You are in deep water, Jeffrey, this is much more than unlawful disposal of the dead and a four-year maximum sentence. If you helped scrub Payne's flat to get rid of any evidence of the murders that took place there, that makes you at least guilty of being an accessory after the fact.' Yellich spoke gently, knowing that softly spoken words can carry much further than words harshly spoken. 'And if you were party to the murders, then you're looking at life.'

'And at your age, Jeffrey, life will mean life.'

It was then that Pinder paled and burst into tears. It was a very nice sight. A very pleasing sight indeed. 'What can I do?'

'Make it hard for yourself, or make it easy for yourself. Up to you. Choice is yours.' Yellich offered Pinder another nail.

'We haven't pulled Payne, or Ismay, or Small, or Hodges, yet.' Hennessey relaxed back in the chair. 'But we know where they are. We'll pull them this afternoon.'

'That's right.' Yellich flicked the lighter and Pinder drew deeply on the cigarette. It was another lie, but it was all part of the game. 'They've got records, we've been keeping tabs on them . . . and we'll be putting the same deal to them. Help us, we'll help you.'

'We get the impression that Payne and Ismay will be difficult to crack, but Tim Small doesn't sound like he'd do well in prison, and I don't think Dorothy Hodges will care for life in the female wing of Durham Prison.'

'E wing, Durham,' Pinder exhaled. 'I've heard of that.'

'Well, it's where you'll be going . . . the question is for how long? And that, Jeffrey, is up to you.'

A silence. Then Pinder said, 'I don't suppose I have a choice.'

'Oh, you do.' Hennessey smiled. 'You can drop them in it before they drop you in it. Think about what Tim Small knows about you, and what Dorothy Hodges knows, because whatever it is, we'll know about it within the next hour or two.'

'Perhaps you could start by telling us who the guy that was buried in your garden was?'

'I don't know, honestly. I think he was a down and out, a dosser . . . he was about James Payne's height. I was in deep trouble with the moneylenders . . . I was . . . they were into me for thousands. If I didn't pay up I was dead. They were going to make an example of me. I was desperate . . . desperate men do desperate things.'

'So I believe.'

'Payne wanted to disappear. He paid off the money-lenders and in return, I allowed him to bury the body in my garden. He brought it round one dark night, him and Izzy . . . just the two of them. If it was found, I was to say it was James Payne and that I had killed him in self-defence, collect a short sentence. If it wasn't found, then all well and good . . . but I was free of the moneylenders. I never saw Payne after that. He'd come out of prison for the robbery, he wanted to make a fresh start, new name . . . but you know where he is?'

'Oh, yes,' Hennessey said, and even Yellich thought he sounded convincing.

'Tell us about the girl who kept a Soundings Ltd pen in her mouth?'

'I didn't know one of them did.' It was an interesting answer: it meant Pinder knew about the murders.

'One did . . . those pens proved very useful. Led us to you, for example.'

'Dorothy Hodges worked for a cleaning company called Steps and Stairs.'

'Yes, we've spoken to them.'

'They cleaned for Soundings and one day the manager gave out handfuls of these complimentary pens, just couldn't get rid of them, so Dorothy got a handful, handed them to us . . . Payne, Izzy, Tim Small. I remember I saw one or two in the flat above the shop. Payne had a writing desk in the living room. I saw a few of them on the desk whenever I visited. Small pens, really small.'

So that was it, thought Hennessey. A girl, restrained or assumed to be unconscious, left alone, seized the opportunity to put something in her mouth that she hoped would lead the police to her abductors, and she did that in the knowledge that she would soon be killed. If a photograph provided by the families matched the skull of the first skeleton to be found, then the police would know which girl had the presence of mind to leave them a present. He only regretted that it had taken twenty years, more in fact, to discover it. Twenty-plus years of agony for the family of each girl . . . the not knowing . . . little, he thought, little could be worse than that.

'So, tell us about the murders.'

Pinder drew on the nail. 'This will help me, yes?'

'It won't hurt you.'

'Might even be good for your conscience,' Yellich added.

'Well, I wasn't there when those lassies were murdered. I helped tidy up afterwards . . . they called me "the dustman".'

'The dustman?'

'I picked up after them.' Pinder shrugged. 'They were already a gang when Payne asked me if I'd be interested in earning some money . . . he must have clocked me for a thief . . . takes one to know one.'

'More than a thief, Jeffrey.'

'Well, bent then . . . twisted in the head . . . still takes one to know one. It was my job to get rid of their belongings. Payne liked to keep the underwear as a sort of trophy, but shoes, jeans, jackets, handbags . . . anything . . . all had to disappear, not just be taken out and dumped, but vanish, and I mean vanish.'

'What did you do?'

'Took any nametags out of the clothing and drove with them out of York and left them in a plastic bag outside the door of a charity shop. That way, if the charity shop wanted them, they'd get mixed up with all the other second-hand clothing, and bought by different folk. Say there was six items of clothing from one girl, those six items could be purchased by six different people in other towns. Usually I went east to Leeds or Bradford . . . one girl's clothing went to Sheffield. If the charity shop didn't want them they would put them out with their own refuse. That way no one would be suspicious, not like leaving a pile of clothing at the side of a layby.'

'Clever,' Hennessey growled.

'Well, I thought so.' Pinder smiled an unpleasant smile. 'Any cash they had went into my pocket, that was the deal, but they were students . . . didn't have more that the price of a night in the pub, not one of them.'

'Poor you.'

'The papers they had in their bags . . . essays and the like . . . they went up in smoke . . . that left their bags and possessions like watches and that . . . everything went into their bag, plus a house brick and went into the Ouse by Lendal Bridge . . . after all this time, they'll be in the mud, well sucked in.'

'Ever see any of the girls at all before or after they were murdered?' Hennessey's distaste for the man grew by the minute. He doubted the authenticity of Pinder's confession . . . that smile . . . he felt it was highly likely that Pinder was far more implicated than he was prepared to admit and Pinder's answer did not surprise him.

'No,' said Pinder, 'I never did. Just the dustman.' He even managed to look Hennessey in the eye as he spoke.

'Did you collect the possessions of the deceased from the murder location?'

'Yes, all neatly put in a pile by Hodges . . . either in the flat above Payne's little shop or from a derelict house out in the sticks.'

'Dorothy Hodges collected the girls' possessions?'

'Yes, everything that Payne didn't want.'

'Payne was the leader?'

'Yes, him and Izzy were like Division One of the gang, Hodges and Small were Division Two . . . and me . . . I was minor counties south.'

'Just the dustman,' Yellich said coldly.

'What do you know about the murders?'

'Only what I figured out.'

'Being?'

'Well, there was no sign of struggle . . . they must have been well overpowered . . . no blood, so they weren't stabbed . . . strangled . . . plastic bag over their heads.' Again he smiled. 'Bet these walls haven't heard anything like this for a long time.'

'You'd be surprised what these walls have heard . . . or maybe, then again, you wouldn't, but you won't be able to tell them anything they haven't heard before.'

'You reckon? Reckon you're right. Anyway, the girls who were murdered in the flat above the shop, they were murdered when they were abducted . . . I think anyway. The girls taken to the old house were kept alive for a day or two . . . I think anyway . . . something that Dorothy

Hodges said, "kept her longer than I thought they would" or words to that effect. But this will help me?'

'If it's true,' Hennessey said. 'We'll get all this down in the form of a statement and ask you to sign it. You'll certainly be charged with conspiracy to murder, after the fact. Five charges.'

'So it's some porridge for me?'

'Quite a lot of porridge, I'd say, but significantly less than you'd be eating if you didn't cough.'

'And you've helped us,' Yellich added. 'We'll let the court know that.'

'What do you think? Ten years, out in five . . . ?'

'Life I'd say,' said Hennessey, sitting in the passenger seat of Yellich's Ford Escort as Yellich drove through the late September foliage of the Vale of York.

'I wouldn't expect too much leniency either, if I were him, statement or no statement. Let the parole board sort his fate out. He might have been frightened of the moneylenders but Payne didn't have a gun to his head. He was their "dustman", as he called himself, for the money. And he did a very good job of it as well. Life with the possibility of parole, I would think.'

'Unless the others implicate him further.' Hennessey glanced over the statement he had taken and Pinder had signed. 'But my old copper's waters tell me that this is the tip of Pinder's iceberg.'

The remainder of the journey was passed in silence.

Upon reaching Micklegate Bar Police Station, Hennessey and Yellich stood side by side checking their pigeonholes. A hand-written note in Hennessey's pigeonhole told of a phone call received from the forensic science unit at Wetherby for his attention. The four photographs of the deceased young women had been matched, one each to each of the photographs of the skulls. Identity was thus proved, the skeletons were indeed those of Joyce Bush of Bristol, Melita Campion of London, Charlotte Philips of Derbyshire and Christine Tate of Liverpool. The note added that the official report would be faxed as soon as possible. It was from a scientist called Toby Partridge, a young man of Hennessey's previous acquaintance. He showed the note to Yellich.

'Four families who can start grieving.' Yellich pursed his lips. 'And at least we have four matches . . . it would be bad for us if one or two didn't match, it would mean there would be more victims. Four is enough, it's quite enough. Now what, boss?'

'Lunch.' Hennessey smiled. 'We have had a good morning. 'Can you come to my office at two p.m.?'

'Certainly.'

Hennessey walked to his office and sat at his desk. He picked up the phone, jabbed 9 for an outside line and phoned the forensic science laboratory at Wetherby. He asked to be put through to Dr Partridge.

'Patridge,' said the eager voice, and Hennessey pictured him in his mind's eye, about twenty-five, balding, bespectacled.

'DCI Hennessey, Micklegate Bar Police Station. I received your telephone message.'

'Oh yes . . . oh good . . . oh yes . . . thought you would want to know as soon as poss. Each photograph could be matched to a skull, no doubt about it.'

'Thanks, that does help us . . . but the skulls have case numbers.'

'Yes . . . each has a case number. Last digit is different – 1, 2, 3 or 4 to the final digit, denotes the order in which the skeletons were found.'

'Good, this is what I want to ask you. What is the name

of the skeleton whose case number ends in 1. In other words, the name of the first skeleton to be exhumed.'

'Alrightee . . . let's see now, she was Charlotte Philips. Oh, yes.'

'Thank you,' Hennessey said warmly. 'Thank you indeed.' He replaced the phone gently. So they had Charlotte Philips to thank for having the presence of mind, and the unselfishness, to pop a small ballpoint pen in her mouth in the hope that it would one day be found and would help to lead the police to her killers. He would ensure Derbyshire police were told of that with the request that her surviving relatives be informed of Charlotte's selfless courage. Then he picked up the phone again, and dialled another outside line. 'Vera,' he said when his call was answered. 'Vera, it's George in York . . . Vera, I have something to tell you.'

Vera Campion had said, 'Thank you, George, I appreciate it. I'll have her home soon . . .' and had put the phone down before, George Hennessey knew, she burst into floods of tears. It was not an easy call to make, but he felt the news was better to come from him than from a uniformed constable calling on her. He settled back in his chair and stared at the phone. The phone call had taken the edge off his appetite but he knew he would need strength for the afternoon. He walked into York and, as was his usual practice, he took the walls, and once across Lendal Bridge, found his fancy inclining to Italian food and so a leisurely meal of lasagne at a small restaurant near Bootham Bar. He returned to Micklegate Bar Police Station feeling the benefit of the food but with his thoughts still dwelling on Vera Campion in her small terraced house in Greenwich. He hoped she had someone to be with, even if it was only a neighbour. At five minutes to 2 p.m. he was again sitting behind his desk. At 2 p.m. precisely, Somerled Yellich tapped on the frame of his office door. Moments later the two men were reading the files on Dorothy Hodges, Tim Small, David Ismay and, with the most interest, James Payne.

Yellich looked at Hennessey. 'Bring them all in?' he asked.

'Not sure.' Hennessey picked up a ballpoint pen and tapped it repeatedly but softly on his desk top. 'Not sure . . . they don't seem to be a gang anymore. You see, I think I'd rather nibble away until we have enough to charge Ismay and Payne. My feeling is that Hodges and Small will belly up and feed us Ismay and Payne in return for reduced charges . . . they'll be middle-aged now . . . burned-out criminals – a long stretch will have little appeal. When they were younger they might well have wanted to do time in order to give themselves street cred . . . we've both come across that attitude . . . but few people over the age of forty think like that.'

'None, I'd say.' Yellich glanced again at the file on Dorothy Hodges, 'Once you get to forty, I would think that you have taken on board the fact that you are time limited and you won't want to waste a single day, let alone the rest of your existence.'

'Would think?' Hennessey smiled.

'Well, I have still to hit forty, boss . . . but, well, I have my life insurance in place.'

'Sensible man . . . so what has Dorothy Hodges been up to of late?'

'Of late, nothing. Not come to our attention for nearly ten years. Last before the York Bench for shoplifting from Marks and Spencer's . . . one year's probation. Last address is on the Tang Hall estate. She's now a.k.a. Wells.'

'OK. Let's pay her a call.'

Chaotic. It was the only word to describe Dorothy Hodges' small flat. Items of clothing were strewn across the floor, the bed was unmade and crumpled, the kitchen was a place of unwashed pots, of bin liners filled with refuse leaning against the wall, six in all, like drunken men outside a pub after last orders had been called. Dorothy Hodges, as Vera Campion had done, looked a lot older than her years. She had a mop of grey hair that hung to her shoulders . . . whiskers grew out of her cheeks, both upper front incisors were missing, she had nicotine stains on her fingers. Yet according to her numbers she was still only forty-five years of age. She had, though, managed to acquire a husband along the way – a wedding band said so. She received the officers with resignation, opening the door upon their second knock . . . tutting with annoyance, turning her back on them and walking back into the flat in a gesture of invitation to enter.

'So, what is it now?' she said with an air of impatience. 'I have to pick up my son from school at three thirty. Whatever it is, I don't know about it. I've been straight ever since I got married . . . my man walked out on me, the marriage didn't last, but I have a son to care for.'

'That would be Mr Wells?'

'Aye . . . and if it's him you're after, I don't know where he is and I don't want to.'

'Pleased to hear that you have been behaving, Dorothy,' Hennessey said, 'but we think you can help us with a little matter which took place when you were not as good a citizen as you are now.'

'Come to dig up the dirt . . . that's not right, that isn't.'

'Well, "digging up the dirt" is quite appropriate,'

Hennessey replied, already feeling more than a trifle itchy in Dorothy Wells, née Hodges' flat. 'Do you watch the news, or read the papers?'

'Don't do neither. Watch TV but not the news and I can't afford newspapers. No interest in the world . . . just get on with my life . . . me and my son, Jason. He's ten.'

'Well, if you had watched the news, you'd have seen a lot about digging up,' Hennessey said calmly.

'But skeletons,' Yellich added, 'not dirt.'

'Four of them.'

'Young women . . . ring any bells, Dorothy?'

But Dorothy Wells, née Hodges, was paling fast, and reached out for the greasy surface of the tabletop to steady herself.

'You're under arrest in connection with the murder of Melita Campion.'

'My son . . . Jason.'

'You're allowed one phone call, I suggest you use it to call the school . . . they'll make arrangements.'

'There's no one to look after him.'

'The welfare people will do that . . . come on . . .' Hennessey put his hand on her shoulder. 'You may as well know that Jeffrey Pinder has coughed in order to negotiate a reduced sentence . . . Have a think in the car – you could do the same. It's really Payne and Ismay we want.'

'I don't owe them two nothing.'

Hennessey and Yellich glanced at each other and smiled. It was all coming down like a house of cards.

'We were this gang.' Dorothy Wells leaned forward in the chair, holding the plastic beaker of coffee in one hand. 'We done people we didn't like, students mostly. They got up Jimmy Payne's nose, all that privilege . . .

We did a lot, never got done for any of them. Got done for breach and assault but they were fights in pubs, couldn't get out of it. Did taxi drivers too . . . hired a taxi, took us out into the Vale, some remote place, did the driver . . . borrowed the cab and drove back to York, but not often. Mostly it was students, a bang on the head, then in with the boot. Mostly it was men students but occasionally they did a lassie student for me. I'm not pretty, never was, but those university girls . . . they've got brains and looks. I used to hate them. Really hate them for it.' She drew on the nail. 'Then Jimmy took a corner shop in Holgate. We were talking one day in the pub and he said he was in his shop . . . just him behind the counter, and this girl walks in . . . student type . . . young, pretty, there was just her and him in the shop. She bought a pint of milk or something then left, but he said, "For a minute she was mine . . . if I had some help I would have had her." Then he and Izzy looked at each other and started to laugh.' She paused. 'Just went from there. Payne would stand behind the counter, me and Tim would be like customers and Izzy was outside . . . not all day . . . just for an hour about five p.m. That's when Payne said the students tended to nip into the shop on their way home. Other times of the day it's pensioners popping in and out. The plan was that if no one else looked like they were coming in the shop and no one else was about, walking past like, then Izzy would follow a girl into the shop, turn the open/shut sign round and pull a screen across the window in the door. That would be the sign for a pounce.'

'Which you did?'

'Yes.' Dorothy Wells began to sniffle. She drew no sympathy from either officer. 'Four times we did it . . . over quite a long period. Payne said we shouldn't do it too often.'

'Then what happened?'

'Bundled the lassie upstairs . . . hand over her mouth . . . took her to an attic room right at the top of the shop. The shop had a ground floor . . . the shop itself . . . then the flat above the shop, then an attic above that. Took her to the attic . . . kept her quiet.'

'Then?'

'Then he opened the shop and did business until closing at about eight. The shop was never shut for more than a few minutes.'

'Then?'

Dorothy Wells paused. 'You can guess the rest. Three guys . . . one defenceless woman.'

'We'll need more detail than that in your statement, if you're going to help yourself.'

'OK. I just want to do what's right, you might not believe me but I just want to do what's right for those lassies.'

'Then they were murdered?'

'Eventually.'

'Eventually? What does that mean.'

'It means, eventually.'

'How long were they kept against their will?'

'Days.'

The interview room fell silent . . . a heavy atmosphere descended on the room. Even the duty solicitor, a man of late middle years, who was provided in observance of the Police and Criminal Evidence Act, and who looked as though he had heard it all before, even he looked as though he was about to be ill.

'Payne and Izzy and Small wanted to keep the flesh alive . . . but they were also frightened of being raided. So the girls were murdered.'

'How?'

'Plastic bag over their head. Payne was frightened of blood being spilled. He said even a microscopic drop of blood could be linked to the girls . . . so, no blood.' She paused. 'But later, just before they were buried, he smashed their skulls anyway . . . just making sure.'

'They were all murdered in the flat?'

'Two were. Two were driven away at night . . . in the back of Payne's little car, taken to a derelict house . . . kept there for a few days . . . all were buried in the same bit of land . . . a waste ground that Izzy had discovered. Payne and Izzy dug the graves at night.'

'Why take them to the derelict house?'

'Payne got scared of them being in his flat. He felt safe with them out of his flat – stupid really. If they were found by someone, they could have told the police how and where they were captured . . . but Payne was the boss.'

'Were you there when they were all killed?'

'Yes, I was . . . at the flat over the shop and after they had buried them, me and Tim had to mark the grave with a white painted brick. Payne told us to do it. Pinder was there too – when the girls were murdered in the flat.' Hennessey nodded. His 'old copper's waters' had been right: Pinder was more deeply involved than he was prepared to admit.

'Do you know where Small, Ismay and Payne are now?'

'Yes.' Dorothy Wells held eye contact with Hennessey. 'Yes, I do.' Hennessey waited.

'Well, Tim Small lives with his mother in a small house on the Tang Hall estate. We're both Tangies.'

'That's the address we have, boss.' Yellich turned to Hennessey. 'He's been quiet for ten years.'

'He's long-term unemployed,' Dorothy Wells said matter of factly.

'Ismay?'

'He did well. Izzy did well, so did Payne . . . proceeds of the robbery.'

'I was going to ask you about the robbery.'

'Well, that's why I'm willing to give them up. We rolled that guy Mowatt for eight hundred thousand quid. It was to be split five ways . . . over a hundred thousand each. Came to the split, Ismay and Payne took the lot.'

'The lot?'

'Practically.' Dorothy Wells gritted her teeth in a display of anger. 'Let me and Tim and Pinder have ten thousand each. The rest was shared between those two, Ismay and Payne. Said ten thousand was enough for us . . . said it was big money for the likes of us but not for those two, so they were entitled to what they took, and they did the rolling anyway. Tim was a spare part in the robbery and Pinder was the wheel man, I was a spare part as well, they said, but me, I gave them the information in the first place . . . overheard the guy talking on the phone while I was cleaning round him with Steps and Stairs. That had to count for something, but it didn't, not with Ismay and Payne. Told us to take the ten thousand and shut up . . . or we'd get a kicking. Tim, he couldn't argue . . . he took his ten and was never out of the bookie's trying to make it grow that way, but the bookie took the lot. I held on to mine, kept it . . . woke up one day and my husband had gone and so had the money . . . about seven or eight thousand by then, but Ismay and Payne . . . they used it.'

'Ismay kept Payne's share safe.'

'Yes . . . Ismay and Payne were like brothers . . . maybe still are . . . or maybe Ismay knew that Payne's silence in the slammer could be bought by keeping his share safe. You can buy a lot of quiet for nearly three hundred thousand quid. Depends how you look at it. Anyway, they used it to go straight.'

'Straight?'

'Ismay is the owner of a string of video rental shops . . .
Yorkshire Video Rentals, that's his company. Set it up
with his share of the robbery money. He's worth a lot
more than three hundred thousand now . . . but Payne . . .
he was fly, he was like a barrel load of monkeys . . . he
did a disappearing trick, left a house empty, left a chain
of off-licences, wanted people to think he disappeared.
If he kept his nose clean he wouldn't be traced to
the murders, so he thought. He's a hotelier now . . .
in Scarborough . . . not the Grand, but not the bed
and breakfast guest house either, nearer the Grand, so
I'm told.'

'Do you know the name of the hotel?'

'I don't . . . but he goes by the name of Last now,
Sam Last.'

'That's been a great help,' Hennessey said. 'Really has.
We'll set this down in a statement.'

'But I've helped myself?'

'Oh, yes . . .'

'It took you twenty years to catch up with us.'

'It took us five days. It took twenty years for a gentleman who drinks too much to remember he watched one
of your victims being murdered and buried on the waste
ground.'

'She went quite calmly to her death,' Yellich said
coldly, 'dragged naked over the ground, into a hole,
whacked over the head with a spade, then covered with
soil. He said they walked away again like they'd just done
a day's work.'

'That's those two.' Dorothy Wells shook her head. 'No
conscience at all, either of them.'

Tim Small was arrested protesting his innocence. David
'Izzy' Ismay was arrested at home in front of his wife

215

and children, all of whom were clearly shocked. He said nothing but didn't resist the arrest. It was, though, the arrest of James Payne that Hennessey recalled most vividly in years to come.

A phone call to the Yorkshire Tourist Office at Scarborough brought the name of the hotel owned by Mr Sam Last. It was a large building, twenty-four bedrooms, set back from the coast in ten acres of landscaped gardens. Hennessey and Yellich reported to the reception desk and were received by a perfectly turned-out brimming-with-confidence hotel manager. He invited them into his office and thanked them for coming so quickly.

'Quickly?' Hennessey remained standing, declining the invitation to sit down.

'Yes, I only reported it this morning. The guests that left without paying, that's what you're here about, isn't it?'

'Frankly, no,' Hennessey said. 'We're here to talk to a Mr Payne about the murders of Joyce Bush, then aged twenty, Melita Campion, then aged nineteen, Charlotte Philips, then aged twenty-one, and Christine Tate, then also aged twenty, the murders being committed in excess of twenty years ago.'

Payne's face fell off. It was the only expression Hennessey could think of to describe Payne's facial expression. His face seemed to expand and then slide off his head, downwards, due to gravity.

'We also want to talk to you about the murder of an unknown person, a down and out whose body was found buried in Jeffrey Pinder's back garden,' said Hennessey. But by then, Payne was slumped in a chair, holding his head in his hands.

Epilogue

The trial of Jeffrey Pinder, Tim Small, Dorothy Wells, David Ismay and James Payne took place at the High Court in Leeds the following summer. All the defendants pleaded guilty. Dorothy Wells received eight years, Tim Small, twelve, Jeffrey Pinder, life, David Ismay, life and James Payne, also life. In the case of the latter two defendants, the stern, red-robed judge said that in their case, life must mean life.

After the trial, George Hennessey revisited Greenwich, London, and he and Vera Campion, each holding a wreath, walked arm in arm to the cemetery.